SEASON OF SECRETS

Wealthy wildlife expert Jeremy Fenner detests gold-diggers. He masquerades as a poor man while he works on a secret project to turn his land into a game park. He is intrigued when landscaper Emma Milton kindly gives him generous terms at cost to her struggling business. But Emma's cousin Antonia wants Jeremy for herself and sabotages the work. What's more, Antonia's father has secret plans to defraud Jeremy of his land . . .

Books by Beverley Winter
in the Linford Romance Library:

HOUSE ON THE HILL
A TIME TO LOVE
LOVE UNDERCOVER
MORTIMER HONOUR
THE HEART'S LONGING
LOVE ON SAFARI
WOMAN WITH A MISSION
BUTTERFLY LADY

BEVERLEY WINTER

SEASON OF SECRETS

Complete and Unabridged

LINFORD
Leicester

First published in Great Britain in 2005

First Linford Edition
published 2006

British Library CIP Data

Winter, Beverley
    Season of secrets.—Large print ed.—
Linford romance library
1. Love stories
2. Large type books
I. Title
823.9'14 [F]

ISBN 1–84617–223–3

Published by
F. A. Thorpe (Publishing)
Anstey, Leicestershire

Set by Words & Graphics Ltd.
Anstey, Leicestershire
Printed and bound in Great Britain by
T. J. International Ltd., Padstow, Cornwall

This book is printed on acid-free paper

1

Professor Jeremy Fenner, renowned wildlife author and world authority on antelopes of the sub-Sahara, tried not to grind his teeth.

He was too much of a gentleman to utter the words which were about to blister his tongue, and clamped his jaw instead, so tightly that he was in danger of fracturing it.

'No, Charlotte,' he gritted, 'I will not marry you before the year is out, despite this being the third time of asking.'

The stunning blonde who reclined in the passenger seat of his metallic blue Porsche gave a trilling laugh, which didn't succeed in hiding her frustration. 'Then you'll just have to get used to the idea of being asked, won't you, darling? This is a leap year, or had you forgotten? It's traditional for a woman to propose to her man.'

'Only on the twenty-ninth of February, which is long past. It's almost September.'

Jeremy's lips tightened. He was not her man! It was incredible how such a beautiful woman could possess the hide of a rhinoceros! She simply would not take no for an answer.

Leap year . . . how could he possibly forget it? Charlotte's attempts were just three of the seven such proposals of marriage he'd had to endure in as many months. Seven confounded propositions from women he didn't even like.

The so-called 'fair' sex, he reflected cynically, were not fair at all. They were dark and devious, whatever the colour of their hair. Fortune hunters, the lot of them, and ruthlessly determined to clean a man out of his inheritance.

He knew he was attractive to women, it would be useless to deny it, but heavens, at least half the young women of his acquaintance seemed to imagine themselves in love with him, and all because of his money.

'Charlotte,' he drawled, controlling his temper, 'I thought I had made our position clear. You and I do not have, and never will have, a relationship of any kind.'

'Give it a little time, darling,' Charlotte purred.

Jeremy's knuckles tightened on the steering wheel. The woman was driving him insane. 'Not ever,' he snapped. 'I have no intention of being inveigled into the matrimonial state by you or anyone else.'

He was too kind a man to add, 'and least of all by my cousin's ex-wife.'

'No relationship?' Charlotte Fenner parried, 'that can easily be remedied.' Beneath all that fluffy femininity she was one very determined lady. 'You can start by removing your elegant nose from all those boring tomes about warthogs, and suchlike. One would think the African bush held the secrets to life itself.'

She reached out and ran her

blood-red acrylic fingertips up his muscled leg. 'There are other animal species in life, you know, and you are allowed to think about them.'

Firmly Jeremy removed her hand. 'Charlotte, you are a beautiful woman and you will one day find a suitable man to keep you happy, but I am not that man. I have no intention of . . . '

'You can't blame little old me for trying, can you? Besides, we already have the same surname. It wouldn't take much to . . . '

'No!'

'If you're concerned about my lousy marriage to Craig, you needn't be. You see, it . . . '

'Ended when his money ran out? That I can well believe.'

Charlotte's perfect complexion mottled with sudden anger. 'That's not true!'

'It is, and well you know it.'

'Jeremy darling,' she begged sweetly, 'let's not quarrel. Let's talk about our future, it's much more exciting, and if you say we don't have a relationship

4

then you may remedy that by taking me out to dinner this evening and we'll take it from there.'

Ignoring his cold, disbelieving silence she tinkled on self-centredly, 'Little Charlotte always gets what she wants, darling, you'll have to get used to that.' Her violet eyes glinted with an unbecoming, avid anticipation, ' . . . and little Charlotte wants you.'

'No, Charlotte, you want my money.'

Her forced laugh ended in a pout. 'You're wrong. What would I do with all that beautiful folding stuff?'

'You'd go through it in less than a year, as you did with Craig's. No, Mrs Fenner, you'll have to accept that I mean what I say. I have no intention whatever of dining with you tonight.'

He glanced in the rear-view mirror before overtaking a large truck which appeared to be ferrying a load of sugar cane to a nearby mill.

'At your request, I have shown you around my new home and now I am driving you back to the coast.' A waste

5

of a day it had been, too. 'After that, I must ask you not to contact me again. Is that clear enough for you?'

Slowly it began to dawn on Charlotte that she wasn't making much headway.

'It's the red hair, isn't it?' she hissed. 'I knew it!'

Jeremy's jaw dropped. 'What red hair?'

'That redhead who passed us as we came out of your drive a while back. She was walking two dogs . . . she's probably a neighbour. You fancy her, don't you?'

Her voice rose in spite, 'I saw the way you looked at her, though what you see in hair like that I can't imagine, it's quite orange. You'll discover she's nothing but a country bumpkin with appalling clothes and no idea how to keep a man happy. You wouldn't know a proper woman if she upped and jumped in your tea!'

'I will not discuss my private life with you, Charlotte,' he grated.

He put his foot down on the

accelerator. The sooner he was out of her unappealing company, the better.

Charlotte's eyes glittered. Jeremy really did mean what he said. He actually didn't want her! Her anger turned to a vicious rage she didn't bother to hide.

'You'll be sorry, you stupid, stubborn man,' she spat, lunging at him with both fists. 'No-one turns down Charlotte Fenner!'

Jeremy uttered a sharp word and flung out an arm to restrain her. Charlotte grabbed a handful of his thick, dark hair and pulled wildly. 'You utter toad,' she shrieked, and slapped him hard across the cheek.

'Watch it,' Jeremy yelled in alarm as the car, still travelling at speed, veered to one side and skidded violently on the verge.

Charlotte's shrieking became a terrified scream as the Porsche spun out of control, somersaulted into the veldt and wrapped itself around the nearest thorny acacia tree.

★ ★ ★

Ten-year-old Arabella, her school bag slung over one shoulder, gnawed thoughtfully at her thumbnail as she trudged up the long drive to the farmhouse.

Should she tell, or shouldn't she? It was such a scary secret that her insides were all quivery. Trouble was, no-one would believe her. Nobody ever believed her.

'Peter said not to tell,' she argued with herself.

If she told them, Emma would say she was making it up, and give her a row. Emma was always giving her a row. Trouble was, she couldn't help having a humongous imagination, could she?

The dogs barked their usual welcome as she reached the kitchen door and shoved it open with her free shoulder. Nice and Naughty, their two terriers, pounced upon her before deciding that the garden was more interesting, whereupon they ran out to chase the plump, grey doves from the acacia trees.

Arabella dumped her school things on the floor. 'Emma!' she yelled, 'Emma, guess what?'

A tall girl with glossy red-gold hair turned from the window. 'Hush, I'm here, Arabella. There's no need to yell.'

She'd been indulging in a moment's idleness, savouring the view of rolling green hills, which bounded towards a vast, grassy plain in the far distance. Commonly known as Riverbush because of the winding river, which watered it, the plain provided nourishment for an assortment of wild life, which lived there, and was reputedly owned by an eccentric old man whom nobody had ever seen.

Emma had always considered that it would make a wonderful nature reserve and tourist attraction, should there be any developers who were not greedily prepared to sacrifice its wild beauty at the altar of financial gain.

She frowned. 'You're late, Arabella.

I've told you not to dawdle on the way home. It makes Gran anxious when you're not here on time, and you know how unwell she is at the moment.'

Arabella apologised, suitably meek. 'Sorry, Emma. Peter and I had things to do. Important things, and we forgot the time.'

Feeling that further explanation was necessary she added hurriedly, using her favourite word of the moment, 'Peter and I have discovered a most humongous secret!'

'Yes, well go and hang up your blazer, please — there's a peg for it in the hall, as you well know. And don't forget to wash your hands either.'

Arabella's face fell. 'Yes, Emma.'

'I've made muffins for tea. Hurry, the kettle's just boiled.'

Her elder sister, Arabella decided crossly as she scuttled into the hall, was a total bossy-boots! It was time she got married and had some children of her own to boss, and then perhaps there'd be a little peace around here. It would mean that there'd be no more muffins, of course, but Emma could teach her how to make them before she went off to get married.

She couldn't ask Gran to teach her because Gran was an awful cook, whereas Emma made the best muffins with chocolate chips in them . . .

Arabella hung her blazer on its hook and took herself to the small cloakroom under the stairs to wash her hands. She dashed back to the kitchen, intent on revealing her secret. Her small face flushed with impish glee. She couldn't wait to see Emma's face!

'Emma, guess what. You know Mr Johnson? Well, he's . . . '

'Have your tea first, Arabella, before it gets cold. Jam or honey on your muffin, or just butter? No chocolate chips today.'

'Um, honey.'

'Have you any homework?'

Arabella screwed up her nose. 'Maths and English composition.' Her eyes brightened, 'but I like making up stories, and I know just what to write about today.'

After gulping thirstily she stuffed her mouth with muffin. 'Guess what, Emma? Mr . . . '

'Don't speak with your mouth full, Arabella.'

Arabella swallowed quickly and tried again, this time a little desperately.

'Someone,' she burst out, 'has bought Mr Johnson's farm, Wozani.'

'Yes, I know. I saw them coming out of their drive a few weeks ago. Anyway, it's common knowledge in Nelsburg that the new owners have been doing some renovations to the house. It was badly in need of it, too. The place must be at least a hundred years old.'

She added milk to her mug and sat down. 'I believe quite a few farms in the area have been sold lately. Strange how it's happened all at once.'

Arabella looked alarmed. 'We're not selling our land, are we?'

'No way. Grandfather's wish was that Tom should eventually have it, and we're just waiting for him to leave school so he can actually start farming the land again. We'll be allowed to stay on in this house for as long as we wish.'

She added thoughtfully, 'Nobody knows the name of the new family at Wozani because they're keeping themselves to themselves, but I daresay we'll all discover it in time.'

Arabella hastily swallowed a mouthful of muffin. Her moment of triumph had finally arrived, and she was determined to make full use of it. She flung out her arms in a dramatic fashion and almost knocked over the milk jug.

'That's what I've been trying to tell you, Emma. I know who the new neighbour is!'

'Oh, I see. Well, who is it, then?'

'The new owner,' Arabella announced, her eyes shining with horrified fascination, 'is a murderer!'

Calmly Emma sipped her tea. 'Don't be silly, Arabella.'

'I'm not being silly. He really is a

murderer, I can prove it. Emma, listen to me! Peter and I saw them putting the body in the boot of their car yesterday, and it was jolly heavy, I can tell you, because the one man nearly dropped it. The body was in a black bin bag just like in that Inspector Weston story I was reading. In fact,' she added with relish, 'we saw them moving two big bags, and I wouldn't be surprised if they're keeping a whole lot more bodies inside the house.'

Emma gave an inward sigh. What was to be done with the child? She had an imagination like a runaway train.

'You will stop this nonsense at once, Arabella,' she said firmly, 'and finish your tea.'

'It's not nonsense, Emma, honestly it's not. Mr Johnson would be horrified if he knew who was living in his old home.' She took another bite of muffin. 'Peter said we should call the new owner Mr Monster and I think it's a jolly good name, don't you? Peter said anyone who kills other people has to be a monster.'

She leapt up and attempted a rather unsuccessful pirouette, hindered considerably by her inelegant black school shoes, and chanted sassily as she wobbled, 'bodies in the bag, bodies in the bag . . . '

This, thought Emma in complete exasperation, was the result of all those horror stories Arabella read under the blankets by torchlight when she thought everyone else was asleep.

'Arabella, you're making me dizzy.'

Rather unsteadily, Arabella plonked herself down again and reached for another muffin.

'I'm a delightful child, aren't I?' She grinned. 'And intelligent, too, at least, Mrs Fletcher says so. Imagine! I'm about to solve a mystery which even the police haven't solved, because if they had, Mr Monster would be in jail by now. I'm going to write about it in my creative writing exercise for tomorrow, and I'll call it 'The Mystery Of The Monster With The Black Bags'. Do you think that title sounds all right? Mrs Fletcher's awfully fussy about titles.'

Emma tried not to smile. For all her nonsense, Arabella was a delightful child. 'Yes, you can be very entertaining at times, love, but you must endeavour to control that fertile little imagination of yours. Write your story by all means, and then we'll hear no more about the subject, OK?'

But far from being satisfied, Arabella frowned as she hauled out her English book. It was just as she'd thought — Emma didn't believe her! The man was a real live killer, for goodness' sake.

'He looks like a monster, too, you know,' she explained earnestly. 'He has a black patch over one eye and a scar on his temple and he doesn't shave, and yesterday he wore a bandage around his head but today he's taken it off.'

She took one look at Emma's face and buried herself in her book. 'All right, all right, I won't say another word.'

Emma began to peel the carrots, her

exasperation evident by the way she scraped them and flung their peels into the bin. She had enough other problems to deal with at present without Arabella's nonsense.

'Try not to dawdle with your homework, Arabella,' she advised shortly. 'You still have your chores . . . the animals are to be fed and the table must be set for dinner.'

Arabella gave a great sigh. 'Yes, Emma.' She fiddled with her pencil and tried her utmost to concentrate but the subject on her mind was far too pressing.

'I'm the only one who knows he's a murderer, you know,' she burst out, 'apart from Peter and Peter's aunt and uncle. She's Mr Monster's housekeeper, and Peter heard her telling her husband all about it. Peter's aunt heard the other man speaking on the phone and he told the person on the other end that Mr Monster had killed a woman. So it really is true, Emma, I swear.'

Emma placed the dish of carrots

inside the microwave oven and clamped her lips for fear she'd say something really fierce. Instead, she took a deep breath and drummed her fingers on the counter as she counted to ten.

'Arabella,' Emma grated, 'be reasonable. How can this man possibly be a criminal? Like you said, he'd be behind bars by now. Anyway, old Bill Johnson would never sell his property to someone who looked the least bit dodgy. It's all a load of nonsense and you are to stop listening to town gossip.'

She poured water into a small silver teapot and arranged the buttered halves of a muffin on her grandmother's tea tray. In an attempt to divert Arabella's attention from the unsavoury subject she seemed determined to discuss, Emma added, 'get on with that homework and then you can take a peek at the kittens in the shed.'

Arabella's frown lifted. 'OK.'

'And don't upset Fatcat with any of that idiotic talk of yours, because she has quite enough on her hands what with feeding those three babies and keeping the mouse population down in the garden shed.'

She left Arabella thoughtfully examining her pencil, and carried her grandmother's tea tray upstairs, setting it down on the small table beside the pink velvet armchair.

'Your tea, Gran, and a nice buttery muffin, freshly baked.'

Mrs Milton set her knitting aside and gave her granddaughter a tired smile. 'You're a dear girl, Emma. Is Arabella home from school yet?'

'Yes, she's busy with her homework. Will you have some of the jam I made from that last lot of strawberries?'

'No, thank you, dear, just the muffin. Has Arabella spoken to you about that new racket yet? You know how mad the dear child is about her tennis. Apparently she's been chosen to represent her house in the inter-house tournament next term, and she tells me your old racket is not really suitable.'

Emma hid her dismay. She said

carefully, 'Arabella did mention it, yes. I'll see what I can do at the end of the month, Gran.'

The old lady looked relieved. 'Thank you, dear. You do so much for us all. If only my pension was a little bigger . . . '

Emma kissed her cheek. 'Darling, you're not to worry about a thing. We'll manage, just as we always have. Now just you concentrate on getting better so that you can take over as chief cook and bottle washer again, and I can return to my life of leisure in the garden.'

Mrs Milton smiled. 'I'll do what I can, dear. It's just that the surgery took a little more out of me than I had expected.' She sipped her tea appreciatively. 'This is nice. What's for dinner, dear? Did you manage to pick up that order from the butcher on your way home?'

'No, but I'll see to it tomorrow.'

Gran, bless her, was not very practical. She had no idea how much the cost of meat had risen, and had recently taken to ordering roasts by the bucket load over the telephone. The order would have to be changed, of course, for the more inexpensive cuts. They'd make do with sausages and ground beef until her next pay cheque came in.

The freezer, Emma thought resignedly, was almost empty. What's more, her bank overdraft had reached its limit and last week the manager had refused her a private loan.

Thank goodness for those late cabbages, and that sack of potatoes in the shed. It would enable her to make mountains of creamed spuds for Tom who was always starving when he came home from high school, especially on the afternoons he stayed late to play rugby.

'Dinner, dear . . . ?' her grandmother prompted.

Emma hid her worries behind a calm face. 'Oh . . . just wait and see. It'll be well worth waiting for.'

Satisfied that her grandmother was

comfortable, she took herself down to the small office near the kitchen and shooed the occupant of the chair out of the door with a crisp, 'off you go, Rascal,' before seating herself at the worn oak desk.

The one-eyed father of Fatcat's kittens departed in a very deliberate manner, his tail held high, so that Emma chuckled as she opened a file on the computer. Her smile soon faded as she viewed the screen, and spent the next ten minutes worriedly doing arithmetic — of a different kind from Arabella's, but just as perplexing.

What were they to do? The miserable thought surfaced that there was only one thing left, and it was something which she'd been steadily refusing to think about for weeks. She would be forced to approach Uncle Harris for a loan.

Her late father's brother would surely have a fair understanding of their financial difficulties, but would he be sympathetic? The thought of asking him for help, however, made her quite ill. She would have to do it secretly, because if Gran knew it would make her ill, too!

'If only my business hadn't slackened off during the winter,' she confided to Rascal, who had just insinuated himself back into the room and was engaged in polishing his face, having recently partaken of a large piece of muffin, courtesy of Arabella.

Although the winter climate was relatively mild around Nelsburg, the gardens took their rest as usual, which meant less work for her. Besides, there was a limit to the number of properties she could maintain, and her salary from her part-time work at Hutchinson's Garden Centre in the town was not solely enough to keep them afloat.

'Cheer up, Emma,' she told herself firmly, 'look on the bright side. Spring is in the air again and it's amazing how much work the growing season can bring.' She simply had to find it.

Perhaps she could put up notices in

one or two shop windows in Nelsburg as she'd done the previous year. There were bound to be newcomers to the town who would like some landscaping or maintenance work done, people like their new neighbour at Wozani, for instance. There'd be no harm in enquiring.

When Emma and her two siblings had been orphaned a few years previously, they had gone to live with their grandparents at Greenhills, where the old man grew vegetables for the local market, but since his death the land had mostly lain fallow.

Emma, being the eldest, had assumed responsibility for the family finances. She'd fought hard to remain in their large, Victorian homestead, knowing it would kill her grandmother if they were forced to sell. So Emma had lurched from month to month trying to make ends meet, and had even abandoned her university course in order to start her garden maintenance business.

In addition, she grew plants and

seedlings in the two large greenhouses behind the house, and sold them at the garden centre. The landscaping part was heavy work, but her brother, Tom, was a great help when she needed him. At present, with his final exams in view, she wasn't keen to encroach upon his time any more than was fair.

Tom came in from school just as Arabella was finishing her maths assignment.

She looked up and blurted, 'Tom, there's a murderer living in Wozani, a real live one, and he looks like a pirate, only Emma won't believe me, and he puts the bodies into black bags, I saw them.'

Her brother reached for the last muffin on the plate and gave her an indulgent glance. 'No, I shouldn't think so, Arabella.' He took a huge bite and winked. 'You know how Emma is, she doesn't believe in fairy tales any more than I do.'

Arabella pouted. 'Tom, I'm serious. Peter's aunt says he killed a woman,

25

and like I said, we saw him putting black bags in his car, so . . . '

'Not now, Munchkin,' her brother cut in, 'I have homework to do.' He went off, still chewing, to his bedroom.

2

A warm wind had been blowing all day, bringing with it the promise of some early spring rain.

Arabella and her classmate, Peter Mazibuko, stepped off the school bus and began the long walk up the hill to their respective homes.

Peter, whose tribe originated some distance away near the Anglo-Zulu war memorial at Islandwana, had come to stay with his Aunt Miriam during term time in order to attend the school in Nelsburg.

'My father works for the Zulu king at Ulundi,' he boasted to Arabella. 'He makes a lot of money.'

'As much as Mr Monster?' Arabella asked, impressed. She added knowledgeably, 'Tom says that to run a car like Mr Monster's means you are very, very rich.'

As they approached the entrance to the farm, Wozani, their footsteps slowed. A delicious shiver played up and down Arabella's spine. 'I wonder if Mr Monster is at home today?'

Peter screwed up his eyes against the wind. 'If that new, fancy blue car's still in the driveway, he'll be there. Let's look over the wall.'

By mutual consent they turned off the road, followed a path to one side of the property and climbed on to a large anthill which gave them their usual vantage point for peering over the wall.

'Inkosi!' Peter whispered in his mother tongue, using the exclamation of awe he'd heard his mother use. 'There's a different car there today . . . and just look at all those black bin bags, they must have piles of bodies in that car!'

Two men appeared in the doorway and strode towards the cream Mercedes parked in the drive. Hurriedly the children ducked their heads, only peering over the wall again when they thought it was safe enough to do so.

They watched, open-mouthed, as the men retrieved the last of the bags from the car and disappeared into the house.

'I wish we could see Mr Monster again.' Arabella sighed.

Peter wasn't about to let her down. 'I know a way to make him come out.'

She squealed in delight. 'Do you? Oh, Peter!' She shuddered. 'He looked pretty cross when he saw us yesterday, didn't he? I don't think he likes children very much. He's a mean, mean murderer.'

'Shh,' Peter warned. 'You mustn't say it so loudly, someone might hear you. Aunt Miriam doesn't know that we know, and I heard her telling my Uncle Isaac that he wasn't to tell anyone else. She said that the poor woman is dead, and nobody can make her come back again. She said Mr Monster should have been put in prison.'

Arabella took a deep breath. 'We'll throw clods at the windows. That'll make him come running outside in a hurry.' She jumped down from the anthill and carefully selected a firm lump of earth. 'Come on, Peter, don't just stand there.'

They spent the next ten minutes flinging earth over the wall. Apart from the fact that neither child could aim very well, the wind had heightened and was interfering rather spitefully with their efforts.

Not only were their faces covered in dirt, but so was the driveway, which included the pristine paintwork on the elegant cream Mercedes.

As expected, the front door of the house flew open and went crashing back on its hinges.

'What the blazes?' a deep voice roared. 'Stop that at once, you children!'

Arabella and Peter, busy collecting clods, hurriedly climbed back on to the anthill and popped their heads over the wall.

They stared, mesmerised, at the tall, angry man bounding towards them.

He was the largest man they had ever seen and looked every inch the fearful ogre they had imagined him to be. His dark brows were drawn together in a frown, there was at least three days' growth on his chin and his dark hair, laced with threads of silver, flapped untidily in the wind. These attributes, together with the scar on his temple and the black patch over one eye, all added to the murderous fury snapping in the other.

'You're a darned nuisance,' he growled, thrusting the hair out of his good eye with one tanned hand. 'I don't need this right now. Clear off, before I get my hands on the two of you!'

Ten minutes later, arriving home in a state of acute excitement not unmingled with fear, Arabella burst into the kitchen and flung herself into Emma's arms. 'Emma! Oh, Emma,' she shrilled, 'we'd better hide!'

Emma, used to Arabella's volatile nature, gently unclasped the child's arms. 'Calm down, love, and tell me

31

what's wrong. Did you have a bad day at school?'

'No, nothing like that . . . it's just that we . . . we saw him again. The murderer, Mr Monster. We saw him and he can't wait to get his hands on us, he even said so. We'd better hide, Emma.'

'Arabella, stop it at once! There is no murderer and he is certainly not out to get us. Now go and hang up your coat and we'll have a nice cup of tea. Would you like a peanut butter biscuit?'

Arabella was close to tears. 'He was grumpy and nasty.' She sniffed. 'And he told us to clear off . . . ask Peter!'

Emma wiped her hands on a tea towel and said slowly, 'Let me get this straight. You and Peter met our new neighbour on the way home from the bus stop and he was verbally abusive towards you?'

'Yes, that's right. He c-can't wait to get his hands on us.'

Emma, usually well in control of her emotions, took a deep breath in order to control her sudden fury. What a beast the man must be to threaten innocent children on their way home from school!

For Arabella's sake she hid her indignation and said soothingly, 'Don't take any notice, love, but if he speaks to you again, please tell me.'

★ ★ ★

Jeremy Fenner ran a hand over his roughened chin as he stared thoughtfully at the departing backs of the two children as they hightailed it up the road. This was the third time in as many days that he'd caught them peering over the wall into his garden, if you could call it a garden, that is. At the moment it resembled the playground of a herd of elephants. However, a bit of dirt flung by a couple of rascals made hardly any difference to the general scene, it was just his new car which bothered him.

With a sigh, he dragged a hosepipe

from the garage and removed the dirt from its sleek, cream sides, reflecting that as soon as he had the time he would do something about the immediate area surrounding the house. He had other plans for the farmland itself, and those could wait.

The garden needed an army of workers to tame the neglected paths and borders, and not only that, but a gifted landscaper who could re-style the whole area. But with the deadline on his current book, the house to sort out and his other land affairs to settle, he'd have to shelve the whole idea until later, just as he'd had to shelve a whole lot of things since the accident. It was time to start living again.

Jeremy returned the hose to its rightful place and went inside to wash his hands. In a short while he would be able to dispense with the eye patch, which would enable him to drive again, but until then he would have to put up with the inconvenience of asking Craig to play chauffeur.

In the living-room his bored-looking cousin flung aside the magazine he'd been paging through. 'Took your time, didn't you? I've made the coffee, but it's probably cold by now. What kept you?'

Jeremy shrugged. 'Couple of kids. They'd covered the Mercedes with soil and I had to clean it off. Nothing serious.'

'Kids? What kids?'

'Oh, just a few locals, I guess. They've been hanging around for the past few days, peeping over the wall, watching me at every turn. Haven't you noticed? I've just sent them packing so I doubt they'll bother us again. What's for dinner, Craig?'

His cousin yawned. 'Steak and boiled potatoes, it's about all I can do. Want to go down to the town for a bite, instead?'

Jeremy shook his head. What Craig meant by that was a night at a bar, chatting up the ladies. They'd only been here a few weeks and already his cousin was getting ready to make a few moves. You'd never think he'd just buried his wife. Ex-wife, that is.

It was still impossible to believe that Charlotte was dead, while he had escaped with relatively minor injuries like bruises and a lacerated eye. The Porsche, of course, had been a complete write-off.

Being in no mood for an evening of frivolity, Jeremy said firmly, 'Steak will do nicely, Craig. I'd like to get back to my work.'

He'd been putting things off for the last few weeks, finding that his normal vitality had considerably abated . . . delayed shock, he supposed. But injuries or no injuries, he must now begin to function again.

'What about those bin bags?'

Jeremy paused at the door. Dash it, he'd forgotten all about them! Why Craig had involved him in something, which was strictly none of his business, he couldn't imagine. But then, he'd always been the one to take responsibility while Craig habitually did as little as he could.

'We'll go through the bags tomorrow and give what we can to the various charities. Charlotte had dozens of everything, so no doubt they'll be pleased to receive all that stuff. Then you'd better notify the removers about her furniture, Craig. The lease on her apartment was due to expire at the end of this month, I'm told.'

Ignoring his cousin's sulky look, he said evenly, 'Thanks for the coffee, Craig. See you later.'

Jeremy disappeared into his partially unpacked study, mug in hand, and closed the door firmly. He stepped over a cardboard box filled with the scientific tomes his late uncle had left him and tried not to spill his coffee. It was to be hoped that his cousin would not overstay his welcome, but on past showing he wasn't holding his breath.

He was fond of Craig, but the man was not, and never had been, his cup of tea. He was self-centred and irresponsible, and it was little wonder that Charlotte had finally divorced him — especially once he'd made that disastrous investment and lost all his money.

Jeremy frowned.

Equally selfish, Charlotte had soon looked around for other fish to fry, and it hadn't been long before she'd tried to hook him, too.

The unfortunate woman had doubtless imagined that Craig's stuffy, absent-minded cousin would make an ideal husband. He was rich, influential and so wrapped up in his work that he'd failed to notice the fun she was having elsewhere. She'd ask him for considerable sums of money, ostensibly for her 'struggling' beauty business, and then proceed over the years to milk him dry.

If there was anything which brought him out in hives, it was a woman who was after his money! And since he'd inherited his late father's estate there'd been more money than he knew what to do with.

Charlotte's funeral, delayed because of the inquest, had been a tiresome occasion, albeit sad. Afterwards Craig had invited himself to stay on the pretext of needing his help to wind up Charlotte's business affairs. He'd suggested that in view of the accident and Jeremy's weakened physical condition, he might be of some help with the move.

Having just endured a spell in hospital and being as yet unsure of whether his eyesight could be saved, Jeremy had been caught at a vulnerable moment, and agreed. How he regretted that decision now, for Craig's sole topics of conversation were women, cars and which thoroughbred was likely to win the next race.

With a sigh Jeremy switched on his computer. Ignoring the fact that his injured eye was still troubling him, he ordered himself back to work. Serious work. By throwing himself into his book again he might just be able to put the last hideous weeks behind him.

Half-an-hour later he looked up, his mind full of sable antelopes, and was amazed to note that a furious downpour was rattling the windowpanes in the study. He rose to close the window, reflecting ruefully that if he'd known it was going to rain he might have saved himself the job of cleaning that car!

He stood peering absently into the garden with his good eye, pondering the opening to his next chapter, when his attention was taken by a schoolboy hurrying up the road. The youth appeared to be heading for the entrance to that small farm which bordered his own land . . . the one he hoped to buy as soon as he could spare the time to approach the owner.

He hadn't met any of the neighbouring families yet, and had no particular desire to do so if his new housekeeper was anything to go by, a Mrs Miriam Mazibuko appeared to be well and truly keeping her distance, darting him wary glances when she thought he wasn't looking, and addressing him with tight-lipped politeness and a wary expression on her round face.

As Jeremy watched, the schoolboy paused and turned to stare at the house. Although in an obvious hurry to get out of the rain, he nevertheless took the liberty of a long, hard look at Jeremy before hurrying on.

'It would seem that I'm blessed with some very strange neighbours. They stare into my garden, chuck mud at my car and generally behave as though I'm carrying a dead fish in my back pocket. Anyone,' he mused, 'would think that Jeremy Fenner was some sort of notorious criminal.'

3

On Saturday morning, Emma eased the old family estate car out of the garage and waved to her grandmother who was sitting next to the bedroom window with her knitting.

'Gran said not to forget to pick up the order from the butcher,' Arabella chirped up from the passenger seat.

After loading the car with groceries and picking up the dry cleaning, they made their way to the bookshop where Arabella darted towards the magazine stand. She found a magazine and darted back, in her haste colliding with a pair of long, muscular legs encased in crisp, navy denim.

'Sorry,' she gasped, and was about to run off when a large hand gripped her by the shoulder.

'Oh, it's you, is it?' Jeremy Fenner said, trying not to laugh. 'Thrown any decent clods recently?'

Arabella's blue eyes widened in shock. 'It's Mr Monster!' she gasped and dived behind Emma's skirt.

Emma looked up and received a small shock. Her heart set up rather an alarming tattoo and her golden brown eyes widened. Apart from the scar and the deplorable lack of a decent shave, the stranger staring at her so intently was an extremely attractive individual, tall and well built, with a distinct macho air which appeared to have frightened Arabella out of her wits.

She propelled Arabella out from under her clothing and strove to keep her voice steady. 'What is it, love?'

'It's him,' Arabella repeated with a shudder. 'It's that horrible man, the one who shouted at Peter and me. He . . . he sells dog meat!' Her small hand, clutching Emma's, trembled. 'He's not wearing his eye patch today but he's still a nasty, nasty man!'

'Arabella, do hush,' Emma implored, beginning to feel a little embarrassed.

'You're quite safe, you know.'

'Well . . . if you say so.'

Arabella glared up at Jeremy and retorted meaningly, 'Carried any decent bin bags recently? Ones with dead bodies in them?'

At last Emma understood. Or at least, part of it. This, then, was their awful new neighbour! Arabella may be speaking nonsense about dead bodies but the fact remained she had been frightened considerably by him. Besides, the children hadn't deserved to be told off in that unpleasant manner.

Emma's eyes blazed. 'You despicable bully,' she accused hotly, 'why don't you pick on someone your own size? If you scare my sister one more time I'll be forced to make a complaint to the police.'

Jeremy stared at her, unable to believe his ears. 'Er . . . bully . . . ?'

'That's what I said. Please understand, that as your neighbours we have no intention of putting up with any more of your miserable, anti-social behaviour.'

Feeling more in control of the situation now, Emma demanded haughtily, 'Your name is . . . ?'

'Fenner,' he drawled. 'Jeremy Fenner.'

Was his brain fogging up, or wasn't it? What in heaven's name was going on here? The belligerent little virago standing before him was stoked up hotter than his grandmother's old boiler. It made a pleasant change from being chased and fawned over.

'May I enquire yours?' he asked politely.

'I'm Emma Milton from Greenhills Farm.'

His gaze sharpened. 'Greenhills Farm?' The very property he wanted to acquire.

He continued to survey her from a great height while he stroked his chin thoughtfully. 'I see. Well, how do you do, Miss Milton. Perhaps you'd be good enough to explain what this is all about?'

'Certainly. My sister tells me that you interrupted her play the other day and told her to 'clear off'! That was most uncalled for Mr Fenner. You're a newcomer to the district and I should like to point out that the children around here are perfectly entitled to throw sand around if they so wish. Kindly mind your own business in future. Goodbye.'

Bright hair flying, she turned on her heel. 'Come on, Arabella, we'll have that tea now at The Chilly Monkey.'

Jeremy continued to observe them as they paid for Arabella's magazine and left the store. Conscious that his mouth was still open, he closed it with a snap. He felt utterly pole-axed on two counts. Emma Milton's extraordinary attack, and her incredible beauty.

He forgot all about the scientific journal he'd intended to buy, and left the bookstore, still pondering over the uncalled-for accusations which had just been made.

Despite the fact that Miss Emma Milton was crazier than a lizard with sunstroke, she intrigued him. It was a long time since he'd found a woman who intrigued him. He returned to his car and sat for a moment in order to savour the unfamiliar feeling.

Jeremy fired the engine, filtered into the traffic and made his way through the town, turning north to the highway which would take him back to Wozani.

He was determined to put from his mind both the Misses Milton, but to his annoyance he found the insidious thought emerging that Emma's glossy curtain of hair remained in his mind.

What was it that strange child had said? Something extraordinary about dead bodies in sacks? A sudden grin tugged at his mouth. Interesting. Even the children here appeared to suffer delusions!

★   ★   ★

The first of the spring rains had brought refreshment to the grassy plain beyond the hills, blessing the tawny veldt with new green shoots to delight the eye, and no less the palates of the wild animals which grazed there.

Emma, driving into Nelsburg a week later, slowed the Volvo in order to gaze at the beauty around her. The sight simply reinforced her conviction that she would never want to live anywhere else, which meant that she was prepared to do anything to safeguard her way of life.

The farm would be kept for Tom who would run it again when the time came, and with the money from any cash crops he grew, life would hopefully become a little easier for them all.

The thought, however, did nothing to lessen the dismay and embarrassment of what she was about to do. After much arguing with herself in the dead of night, she had finally decided to take her courage and approach her uncle for financial help.

At the imposing gateposts Emma idled the engine as she reached for the intercom button, aware that she was being monitored inside the house on closed-circuit television. On being invited by a servant to give her name, she announced brightly, 'It's Emma Milton. I have an appointment at nine-thirty.'

The gates swung open.

'Good morning, Maria,' she greeted the housemaid who opened the door, 'my uncle is expecting me.'

'He is not here,' the woman replied sullenly, not bothering to return her greeting. 'He said you must go to his office.'

Emma blinked. 'But he distinctly told me to come to the house this morning because he doesn't go to the office on a Saturday. He said I was to come early, and I have.'

The maid shrugged. 'It's none of my business.'

'Is Miss Antonia in?'

'No. I heard her telling the master that she wanted to go to the office today, so they went.'

'I see. Well . . . thank you.'

Nothing's changed, thought Emma

as she turned the car and renegotiated the drive. The staff were as unhappy as ever and Uncle Harris was still completely under his daughter's thumb.

She found a parking space outside the offices of Milton & Stanley, Solicitors, soon to become Milton, Milton & Stanley, Solicitors. Her cousin, Antonia, had recently completed an honours degree and was studying for her diploma in legal practice, after which she would join her father.

'Come in, come in,' Harris Milton ordered impatiently when he saw who it was. He didn't bother to rise from his desk. 'What can I do for you, girl?'

'Good morning, Uncle Harris. I've come about a matter of some concern to me, and I thought you may be willing to help ... ' Her voice trailed off uncertainly.

He waved her into a chair. 'I'm extremely busy, but fire away. You don't mind if your cousin is present?' He blazed with pride, 'Antonia will be the youngest trainee solicitor in the province, you know. She's quite brilliant.'

Emma murmured suitably, hiding her annoyance. There was no way she wanted Antonia to witness her misery, however well hidden. On past showing the wretched girl was not above storing all the details in her elegant little head and then pulling them out again when she wished to be spiteful.

'I'd rather not, Uncle Harris,' she said firmly. 'What I have to say to you is confidential.'

'Too late, dearie, I'm here, and I already have your file out,' Antonia purred from behind, closing the door with a snap. She smiled her plastic smile, sashayed to the desk in her five-inch heels and tossed a folder towards her father.

'File? What file?' Emma demanded.

'Oh, I've decided to keep a file on you.'

'But there's no need . . . this isn't a professional consultation. I'm family!'

'Poor relation,' Antonia corrected her

with barely concealed contempt. 'Don't worry, darling, it's nothing personal.'

She perched on the edge of her father's desk and examined her perfectly manicured fingernails. 'I like collecting details, that's all.'

'Quite rightly so, Antonia,' her father beamed, 'takes great pains with everything. In consequence, she will go a long way.'

She smiled at Emma and informed her sweetly, 'I shall start in the court department first, you know. I intend to do really well in the profession and get as high up as I can. In no time I'll be making a name for myself.'

Her sweetness turned to sudden mockery. 'What a pity you gave up your university studies, Emma. You'll regret it, of course. Unlike you, I shall be extremely wealthy, like Daddy.'

She twittered on until her father felt compelled to intervene, albeit reluctantly.

'Exactly, darling . . . but we must get on.' He frowned at his watch. 'I can give you five minutes, Emma, no more. I have another client shortly, an important one, and then Antonia wishes to discuss one of our other briefs before lunch. What is it you wished to say?'

Emma took a deep breath. Hateful as the situation was, it was now or never. 'I'll not keep you long,' she began quietly, determined not to beg. She explained the matter quickly and objectively, hoping that her uncle would be understanding enough to help them in their hour of need. Gran, after all, was his own mother.

Conscious that her cheeks had become rosy, she asked him to consider granting her a personal loan, to be repaid with interest as soon as was possible.

Ignoring her uncle's look of pained surprise, she plunged on. 'I intend to expand my business . . . as I earn more, our lives will become easier, but this will take time . . . the loan would tide us over . . . ' her voice petered out miserably.

'Go to your bank,' Antonia snapped.

'I have, but the manager has refused my application.' Emma's cheeks were now scarlet.

At last her uncle found his voice. 'In that case, there is nothing more to be said, is there? My good friend, Thomas Murgatroyd, is a shrewd judge of these matters, Emma. He obviously considers your enterprise a risk or he would have looked upon your application more favourably. I wish you had not appealed to him, girl, it is most embarrassing for your relations.'

His next words left Emma speechless. 'You have been an extremely foolish young lady! Your father was one of the finest academics in this country and he'd be turning in his grave if he knew what a disappointment you are. As Antonia has so rightly pointed out, you abandoned your university studies and now you must take the consequences. I cannot help you.'

He stood up. 'Goodbye, my dear. Try to manage your affairs more successfully in future.'

'And don't come begging again,' Antonia retorted. 'It's degrading for Daddy.'

Emma marched from the office, her back very straight and her chest heaving. It was the mistake of the century to have come. Thank goodness she'd kept her visit a secret from Gran, the old lady would be livid if she knew. She was livid herself, and mortified beyond measure.

Despite herself, Emma's eyes filled with tears.

'May I?' a masculine voice enquired calmly. It was a voice she had heard recently, a voice like deep velvet, and yet it evoked something unpleasant for her. She peered up at him through a watery mist and her eyes widened. What was he doing here?

'Wh-what . . . ?'

'I said, may I offer you my handkerchief?'

Fiercely she dashed the tears away with her hand. 'No, thank you, Mr

. . . er, Fenner, I have my own.' She scrabbled in her pocket, blew her nose and looked around for the nearest stone to hide under.

She peeped at him through her thick, drowned lashes, her attention drawn once more to the tiny scar beside his left eye. It in no way detracted from his good looks, but rather, made him more appealing in a rugged sort of way.

He'd decided to dispense with the beard, too, and it changed his appearance completely. No longer was he the sour, unkempt pirate of Arabella's description but a handsome, distinguished man in a sober business suit and tie.

Jeremy was gazing at her with a mixture of interest and tenderness. Being a compassionate man at heart, he found that Emma's eyes, soft as a wounded doe's, were quite irresistible. The girl was a complete flake, but she was clearly in some kind of emotional pain and it behoved him, as a reasonable human being, to offer his help.

Strong, tanned fingers fastened on her arm. 'You're upset. Why not sit down for a few minutes? Shall I ask for a cup of tea?'

Emma yanked her arm away. 'No, thank you,' she said stonily. She couldn't leave the offices of Milton & Stanley, soon to be Milton, Milton & Stanley, soon enough.

She heard Antonia's Gucci heels clip-clop across the foyer behind her, and turned in time to see her cousin's eyes widen when they fastened upon Jeremy.

'Jeremy Fenner? How simply lovely to meet you,' Antonia gushed.

With a graceful movement not lost on Jeremy, she reached up to ensure that her perfectly-styled chignon was in place, conscious that its expensive highlights were gleaming golden in the sunshine which streamed through the window.

'Do forgive the lack of a receptionist,

but we're normally closed on a Saturday,' Antonia continued. 'Daddy likes to play golf, you know. He's chairman of the Country Club.'

She flashed her brilliant smile. 'Of course, we had no hesitation in working today when we realised that a famous author and conservationist was our new client. You are an authority on antelope, I believe?' Antonia had done her homework.

With a malicious glance at Emma's departing back, she ushered him into her father's presence rather as though the latter were royalty. 'Do come this way, my father is pleased to receive you now . . . '

Jeremy greeted Harris Milton in a business-like fashion, hiding his feelings behind a bland expression. He'd never normally have consulted a man as unscrupulous as this, but had his own reasons for doing so now. He studied the rather overweight man behind the desk through narrowed eyes and felt nothing but distaste. So this was the jerk who was trying to do him out of his inheritance!

Jeremy's own solicitor, a close and trusted friend, was engaged in handling the purchase of all the new land he had been at pains to acquire of late. It was most unfortunate that Milton was the very person who owned the farm he now needed to complete his property portfolio. After that, the farms would all be incorporated into one estate for the purposes of his secret project.

When the time was right, Jeremy intended to demand from Harris Milton what was rightfully his, and with any luck the affair could be handled discreetly. Like his late godfather, he shunned publicity. Embezzlement was an ugly word, and the tabloids would have a field day if they knew . . .

Antonia, eyeing Jeremy with interest, offered refreshments, which he declined. She chatted knowledgeably for a few minutes about legal matters while her father preened.

Finally Harris stirred himself. 'How

can I help you?' he repeated.

Without hesitation Jeremy told him. 'I believe you are the owner of the land which borders my own farm, Wozani, the farm known as Greenhills.'

'Who told you that?' Harris asked sharply.

'My cousin, actually. He took it upon himself to make some inquiries in the town last evening.'

'Then he's misinformed,' Harris snapped. 'The property belonged to my late father who passed it into the hands of my mother. I regret to say she is a most incompetent and unbusiness-like woman.' Harris frowned as though it were Jeremy's fault. 'Why do you ask?'

'I would like to purchase the property.'

Harris's lips thinned. 'I'm afraid I cannot help you. I believe my mother would be most unwilling to leave the home she came to as a young bride. However, were she to die, the land would be mine and I would certainly consider selling. It's of no use to me.'

Jeremy nodded. 'I understand. In that case, I would not be party to turning an old lady out of her home.' He rose. 'I will not trouble you further.'

Antonia showed him out, all grace and charm.

As Jeremy drove out of town he allowed himself a small grin. It had been comical to watch the girl showing off her newly-acquired legal knowledge while her father had sat like a dazed owl beholding the brilliance of the moon. She'd even tried to discover the exact nature of his enterprise, but he'd been purposely vague. There was no way he would jeopardise his project by telling the Miltons of all people!

Antonia, he remembered, had been secretly amused when he'd mentioned Greenhills Farm, and he wondered why. How incredible it had been to discover she was related to that weepy little spitfire he'd offered to help in the foyer. The two cousins couldn't be more unalike . . .

Craig was just leaving as Jeremy

nosed the Mercedes in the double garage. He leaned from the window of his yellow sports car.

'I'm off to the races at Greyville,' he informed Jeremy. 'I want to be there for the two forty-five . . . had a couple of good tips from a chap in the bar yesterday.'

'Well, drive safely.'

'Oh, I will, I'm not reckless.'

Jeremy ignored the jibe. Craig knew as well as he did that the accident, which had killed Charlotte, had not been the result of his reckless driving, the coroner had made that clear with his verdict.

'I'll spend the night in Durban with friends and drive back some time in the morning,' Craig added. 'I'm having lunch at the Country Club tomorrow with a stunning blonde I met at a fabulous party last night.'

Jeremy nodded absently. Craig was always meeting stunning blondes at fabulous parties.

Craig was watching him through

narrowed eyes. 'She told me that you would be interviewing her father in the morning . . . the solicitor, Harris Milton. You didn't say a word to me about it.'

'No.'

Craig shrugged. He'd no real interest in Jeremy's affairs anyway. The man was a total bore.

'A real doll she is, make no error,' he continued enthusiastically. 'Name's Antonia. Did you meet her, then?'

'I did.'

'And . . . ?'

Jeremy looked bland. 'One blonde is much like another.'

Craig misread the look. 'Well, she's mine, and don't you forget it.' He fired the engine, making more noise than was strictly necessary. 'I'll be off, then.'

He slammed the car into gear and winked as he imparted one final piece of information.

'Her old man's got green stuff by the truck load, Jeremy, enough to buy an oil well. And Antonia has a trust fund coming to her in a year or two from her late mother. Makes the girl all the more attractive, don't you think?' He revved the engine once more and took off down the drive.

'Not in my book,' Jeremy muttered.

In fact, it was a distinct turn-off, almost as much as when the boot was on the other foot and some poverty-stricken woman wanted him for his inheritance. Heaven preserve him from money-minded females of one type or the other. They brought him out in a rash!

Would he ever be able to find a decent woman, a woman of integrity who loved him for himself and not for what he could give her? He had a good mind to go undercover as a pauper to see if he could find such a paragon.

4

Emma drove to her job at Hutchinson's Garden Centre worrying about money. Now that her uncle had refused to help them, there was only one thing left, she simply had to find more gardens to maintain.

It would mean working harder than ever, but it was only for the next few months until Tom had finished his schooling, and then he'd be free to help her with the heavier labour.

Trying to look on the bright side, she told herself that soon there'd be the farm fields to till and the cash crops to plant, and the tomatoes to bring on in the greenhouses. Hopefully when the vegetables were ready, market prices would still be good. The supermarket in Nelsburg would probably take some of their lettuce . . .

In her basket on the passenger seat of

the Volvo were half a dozen attractive little notices she'd spent the previous evening illustrating. After work she would put them up around the town in order to advertise her gardening services.

She knew something was wrong the moment she entered the shop. 'What is it, Lucy?' she asked.

Lucy Hutchinson, niece of the owners, looked up, her eyes red from weeping. 'Bad news,' she gulped. 'My uncle passed away last night . . . heart attack. My aunt's in a state, and the shop is to be closed until further notice.'

Emma stared at her in shock, unable to utter a word.

'A buyer for the business will have to be found, but that will take some time. In the meantime I'm to send any remaining plants to the florist's, and the rest of the stock will have to go the auctioneer's.'

She sniffed. 'I was just waiting for you to come in so I could tell you, then

I'm to place a notice in the window and lock up.'

Emma found her voice. 'I'll make us a cup of tea first, and then help you. I really am really sorry to hear this, Lucy.'

'What will you do? About work, I mean.'

Emma smiled brightly. 'Oh, I'll find something, don't worry about me. In fact, I'm about to expand Greenhills Garden Services ... I've even made some posters for the town.'

'We're to receive a month's pay in lieu of notice,' Lucy thought to inform her. 'Your cheque will be in the post.'

Emma gave an inward sigh of relief. She must be grateful for small mercies.

She drove home after distributing her posters and resolved to make a concerted effort in the next few days to drum up more work, even if she had to go from door to door asking for it.

Arabella was full of the news of Mr Hutchinson's death when she arrived home from school, having heard it at

67

the bus stop from Lucy's younger sister.

'I don't think he died of a heart attack at all,' she stated. 'Peter and I think Mr Monster killed him. We knew something like this would happen sooner or later.'

Emma, having had a stressful day, lost her temper. 'Arabella,' she roared, 'be quiet, or I shall send you to your room!'

Arabella's eyes widened. 'Yes, Emma,' she muttered, and for once went to wash her hands without being told. Goodness, Emma was in a foul mood today. Was it something she'd said?

★   ★   ★

By the end of the week no new customers had been found. Emma was anxious about the bills which were beginning to pile up, and there were more seeds to purchase if she was to have annuals for her clients' gardens in a few weeks' time. The garden shop would no longer be taking her seedlings and she would have to find other outlets for them, possibly in the next town.

Gran needed new slippers, too. She'd just begun to walk again and couldn't manage to wear her shoes yet.

'Is something bothering you, dear?' her grandmother asked her when she took in the tea tray. 'You've been looking a little peaky all week. I'm glad you've decided to leave Hutchinson's, it'll be easier for you. You're not working too hard in the garden, are you, dear?'

Emma, whose arms ached from the vegetable patch she'd been digging over, declared stoutly that she was just fine.

'What colour slippers would you like, Gran?' she asked quickly, changing the subject. 'I'm going in to Nelsburg tomorrow morning for the groceries, as usual. I'll get them then.'

'Blue would be nice, dear, for a change.'

'Blue it shall be,' said Emma,

crossing her fingers behind her back. If she could find enough special bargains at the supermarket, she'd be able to use some of the allotted grocery money.

On Monday, Arabella arrived home from school with yet more news. During the night, Peter's Aunt Miriam had been rushed to the hospital in Durban.

'She had this humongous pain all day yesterday, and now they're going to cut her insides out,' she informed Emma with relish. 'Peter says she won't be able to walk properly for weeks and weeks afterwards.'

'Oh, dear,' Emma murmured distractedly as she tried to decide between spaghetti and macaroni for dinner.

'Peter says his Uncle Isaac told Mr Monster all about it this morning, because Mrs Mazibuko won't be able to work for him any more. At least, not until she's well again.'

'Uh-huh.'

'Do you think he'll be able to find anyone else to work for him? I mean, being a murderer and all that, nobody'll want the job, will they?'

'Arabella, the man's name is Mr Fenner, nor Mr Monster, and he is not a murderer. How many times must I say it?'

'It's not Mr Fenner, it's Professor Fenner.'

Emma stared. 'However did you know that?'

'Oh, Peter told me. The professor's very clever and he writes books and he knows all about wild animals, and stuff.'

'I see.'

'We think he's rich, too. Peter and I think he makes lots of money from that dog meat.'

'Don't talk nonsense, Arabella.'

Arabella gulped her tea thirstily. When she had breathed she added, 'Peter says he's not as bad as we thought he was. He was quite decent about Mrs Mazibuko not being able to work, and Peter says his Uncle Isaac quite likes Mr Monster now.'

Craig's face was like thunder. 'What do you mean, Jeremy, we'll have to do our own housework? What are you paying the woman for?'

'Mrs Mazibuko is on sick leave, and I haven't time to go around finding housekeepers. If you don't like it, Craig, you can always move out.'

Quickly Craig changed his tune. 'Oh, I'm sure we can manage, Jeremy. I wouldn't like to go back to civilisation just yet, I'm just getting to know Antonia Milton.'

Jeremy gave an inward sigh. Getting rid of Craig was not going to be easy. 'Then you may start by taking out the garbage.' He hauled the vacuum cleaner from its cupboard. 'I'll do the carpets.'

Much as he sympathised with his housekeeper's plight, she couldn't have chosen a worse time to become ill. He had precisely two weeks left until that deadline for the publisher, and having wasted enough time on Charlotte's affairs already, wasn't exactly pleased to have any further delays.

They were sitting down to their tasteless pre-packed television dinner of chicken pie supplemented with Craig's boiled potatoes when the telephone rang.

'Antonia wants me to take her out to dinner,' Craig informed him a moment later. Quite shamelessly he emptied his uneaten meal into the bin.

'And you jump to her every whim,' Jeremy observed dryly.

Craig wasn't in the least offended. He winked. 'Sure. I know where my future lies. She's an heiress, remember.'

'Craig, you're beyond redemption!'

'Who cares, as long as I get what I want? You won't believe the things Antonia tells me, Jeremy. You know that redhead next door? Well, it happens to be her cousin.'

'I'm aware of that.'

'Well, you want to keep out of her way, buddy. Girl's a money-grabber! She tried to touch Antonia's old man for some cash recently and he quite rightly refused. Antonia says her cousin will do anything for money, even dig in other people's gardens.'

He went off, whistling, to change his clothes. What Antonia didn't know, of course, was that he'd do anything for money, too, even take her out at the drop of a hat when he knew full well what a spiteful little cat she was. Still, beggars couldn't be choosers, could they? If he sponged on his cousin a while longer and played his cards right in the romance department, he'd soon be rolling in dough. That would put the insufferable Jeremy well and truly in his place!

Satisfied with the way his life was going, Craig climbed into his sports car and roared down the drive.

He returned much later that same evening, filled with gin-induced bon-homie, and peered around the study door.

'What! Still working, Jem, old lad? You'll grow old before your time. You need to find a female and have some fun. You're nothing but a stuffed shirt.'

'And you, my friend,' Jeremy replied coldly, 'are ticking nicely. Go to bed.'

'All in good time. There was something I wanted to tell you, first.' Craig swayed a little on his feet, ' . . . Oh, yes, I remember. You know that female, I was telling you about?'

'What female?'

'The redhead from next door . . . Antonia's cousin.'

'What about her?'

'She's man-mad as well as being money-mad, Antonia said so. She said to warn you so you'd keep a wide berth, because she wouldn't like you to become entangled with a girl like that.'

'I'm touched at her concern for my welfare,' Jeremy drawled.

'I told her she had nothing to fear as you weren't much interested in romance anyway. I said you were so dull you couldn't even attract a dragonfly.'

'Goodnight, Craig,' Jeremy interrupted firmly.

Craig tottered off. 'See you,' he mumbled.

Jeremy closed his computer down and sat for a moment in thought.

Emma Milton may well be a mercenary, ruthless hunter of masculine prey. She may well be crazy, and all that he despised in a woman. And yet his instincts told him otherwise. But could he trust them?

★ ★ ★

Peter and Arabella stood at the gate and stared hard at the house. 'I'm scared,' Arabella confided.

Peter puffed out his chest. 'I'm not. My uncle says Mr Monster is a nice man, Arabella. He said I must deliver the letter on my way home from school because it's important, it's about my Aunt Miriam. Come on, just follow me, I'll go first and ring the bell.'

Arabella tossed her spiky plaits over her shoulders, not quite convinced. Besides, Emma had given her two pigtails today and she wasn't quite sure that they suited her. What if Mr Monster didn't like them, and chased her away?

As they reached the front door Jeremy came round the corner of the house, having been outside to ensure that the workmen who were renovating his home had taken all their clutter with them.

He looked surprised to see them. 'Hello there, kids.'

If the greeting was a trifle absent, it was because his thoughts were already on the last chapter of his book. 'What can I do for you?'

Arabella stared at him with her mouth hanging open. He didn't look at all like a monster today. He looked like a professor, vague, but friendly, and for once his hair was neat. He even had a smile on his face. Perhaps he was a nice kind of murderer, after all, not a horrid kind.

'I've come to deliver a letter from my Uncle Isaac,' Peter explained boldly, handing over the envelope.

'Ah. Mrs Mazibuko. How is she?'

'She's still in the hospital in Durban. She said she's not coming back to work for you ever again.'

'Oh?'

Jeremy slit open the envelope and quickly read the enclosed note. 'I see. Well, thank you for telling me.' He sighed. 'It seems I shall have to find a permanent replacement for her as soon as possible. This housework lark is beginning to pall.'

He pocketed the envelope and roused himself to be hospitable. The children looked hot, having toiled all the way up the hill with their schoolbags.

'Would you kids like some juice and a few chocolate biscuits?'

Already ready for food, Peter beamed. 'Yes, please.'

Hesitantly Arabella followed, her eyes huge as she gazed about her en route to the kitchen. There was an awful smell of paint about the place . . . and not one black bag to be seen. The carpeting had

78

been ripped up and Mr Monster appeared to have hardly any furniture. The living-room had only two chairs and a television in it, and he couldn't even afford a table for the dining-room.

The kitchen, she noted with disapproval, was a mess. Dirty plates cluttered the sink and the tiled floor looked as though it hadn't been washed for days. Mr Monster was about to give them a smashing tea, though . . . chocolate biscuits, guava juice and a little silver dish of peanuts.

'Emma loves housework,' Arabella said suddenly, through a mouthful of beanuts. 'Shall I ask her to help you?'

Jeremy looked startled. 'I beg your pardon?'

'Emma. She's my sister.' Arabella munched happily before enlightening him further. 'She's a dear, but she's twenty-two going on seventy-two, if you know what I mean. And you must never say that her hair is ginger or she'll chew you up. It's 'auburn', OK? Can you remember that?'

She drank thirstily from the large glass Jeremy placed beside her and added, 'We live on the farm next door.'

Jeremy blinked. The child had his full attention now. 'Oh, you mean Emma Milton? You're her younger sister?' Why had he not recognised the strange child who'd thrown dirt at his car and accused him of hiding dead bodies in black bags?

'Yes. I'm Arabella Milton. I'm very intelligent,' she informed him matter-of-factly. 'My teacher says so, and I'm going to write books when I'm older.'

Jeremy hid a smile. 'How nice.'

'Do you like my pigtails?'

Solemnly he viewed the stringy pieces of hair tied with enormous navy blue ribbons and said what was obviously required of him.

'They're . . . er, very attractive.'

Arabella gazed at him with sudden pity. 'You're not very well off, are you? You have no kitchen chairs. There's a shop in Nelsburg that sells second-hand stuff,' she offered kindly. 'We got ours there. Perhaps they'll let you have some now and you can pay for them later, when you have the money.'

Not a muscle on Jeremy's face moved.

'Well,' demanded Arabella when he seemed to be considering things for far too long. 'Do you want Emma or not?'

'It's very kind,' he managed gravely, 'but I'm sure I'll manage, thank you.'

Arabella looked about her sadly. 'You don't look as though you're managing, you know. There's dirt on your fridge door. Shall I clean it off for you?'

She grabbed a dish cloth, wet it under the tap and proceeded to rub the surface clean.

Jeremy watched her, his eyes gleaming with laughter. 'Thank you, Arabella,' he said gravely. 'You've been a great help.'

Arabella helped herself to another chocolate biscuit and crammed half of it into her mouth while Peter finished the rest of the juice before deciding regretfully that it was time to go.

'Come on, Arabella. Thank you for the tea, Mr Monster.'

Jeremy choked. 'Mr who . . . ?'

Peter went red. 'Um, we call you Mr Monster, Arabella and I. We thought, you see . . . ' he trailed off, embarrassed.

Arabella, quite undaunted, came to his rescue. 'We thought you were an awful man but you're actually quite nice, now that we know you.'

She added thoughtfully, 'We'd better change the name, hadn't we, Peter? We'll have to think of something else.' She screwed up her nose with the effort. 'I know! May we call you 'Jolly Jeremy' instead?'

Jeremy gave a bark of laughter, the first in many weeks. It was a long time since he'd been so vastly entertained. 'You may, Arabella, if it makes you happy.'

'Then goodbye, Jolly Jeremy,' Arabella told him, holding out her hand, 'it was a lovely tea, but I'd better hurry home now because Emma will be waiting to give me more tea and she gets crabby if I'm late. Like I said, seventy-two . . . '

At the door she cocked her head to one side. 'I'm sorry you're so hard up, but don't worry, we are too, even though Emma thinks I don't know.'

As Jeremy saw them to the gate, Arabella pointed to the wreckage which was his garden and advised sternly, 'You ought to do something about all this mess, Jolly Jeremy.'

'Yes,' he agreed meekly.

'Shall I ask Emma to fix it for you? Emma likes fixing gardens, she can fix anything. She even fixed the kitchen tap once when we couldn't afford a plumber. I'll tell her to do it for you cheaply, don't worry. I thought you were rich but I can see you don't have very much money, like us.'

'Er . . . no thank you Arabella, I have the matter in hand,' Jeremy managed, trying not to laugh.

Jeremy watched them disappear up

the drive. It was a full ten minutes before he could stop laughing.

The days were warming up considerably and the veld breezes had begun to carry with them the heady scents of early summer.

As the butterflies and bees appeared, Gran watched them with delight from her armchair next to the window. Her feet were much improved and she was looking forward to being able to ramble in the garden once more. The only item of concern to her at that moment was Emma. The girl was looking more strained by the day. Perhaps she should suggest a tonic.

Emma, in fact, was ready to spit. It was two weeks now and there had been not one single response to her advertisements, and what's more, two of her usual clients had phoned in to say they no longer required her services. One was moving away from Nelsburg and the other had decided to maintain his own garden instead.

'What are we going to do, Tom?' she

demanded. 'We still have our other gardens to maintain but it really isn't enough . . . ' she broke off as a lump of frustration rising in her throat made further speech impossible.

Her brother dug his spade into the potato patch he was weeding and wiped dusty hands on his trousers before clapping her on the back.

'Don't worry, Emma. I meant to tell you, I've managed to get us some more work.'

Emma blinked away the sheen of moisture which had filmed her eyes, so that Tom wouldn't notice. 'Oh?'

'I took the bull by the horns this morning when you were shopping in Nelsburg and approached that chap down the road. He said he'd be happy for you to give him a quotation so I said you'd be along as soon as you could, possibly this afternoon, even though it's Saturday.'

He added, 'His garden looks like a rubbish dump.'

Emma's day brightened miraculously.

'That's great, Tom. Which chap?'

'Professor Fenner. You know, the new owner of Wozani.'

Emma was appalled. 'We can't work for him!'

'Why not?' Tom demanded. 'Seemed a decent enough type to me, despite all that nonsense of Arabella's about his being a criminal, or whatever. You know how she imagines things all the time.'

He resumed his digging and confided. 'We had a long chat. He's awfully interesting, knows a lot about wildlife. He asked what you did, and I told him about the business. I mentioned we were actually looking for more work because you'd been made redundant from the garden shop.'

Emma blushed scarlet. 'Tom, you didn't!'

'What's wrong with that? We can't be too proud, love. We need the money if we're to survive until Christmas.'

Emma swallowed. 'Yes, I suppose so. I'll go and see him after lunch. Thank goodness you'll be free to take over the market gardening side of things in the new year.'

Tom's face went blank. 'I guess so.'

'Tom, you really do want to be a farmer, don't you?' she asked anxiously. 'Gran has said the land is to be yours, as you know, but — '

'Of course I do,' her brother interrupted stoutly, hiding his disappointment. How could he disclose the secret he carried night and day? Much as he enjoyed planting things and watching them grow, what he wanted most of all was to be a game ranger, caring for Africa's great heritage, its wildlife.

'Don't worry so, Emma,' he said cheerfully, 'when the time comes I will shoulder all my responsibilities just as I'm expected to.' He'd do so without complaint, too, because now that Grandfather was gone the women were depending on him, and the welfare of his grandmother and sisters must come first.

Emma glanced at her watch. 'I'd better check the stew.'

Once she was out of sight Tom chuckled. What he hadn't yet told her was something she'd find out soon enough, because if he knew Arabella, she couldn't keep a secret for long.

According to Professor Fenner, their incurable younger sister was now his greatest buddy and had taken to visiting him after school in order to advise him about his décor. If Emma knew the professor had now become Arabella's flavour of the month, she'd have a fit!

5

Jeremy was intrigued to find that Arabella's visits had become the highlight of his week.

'Charming child,' he murmured as he went into the kitchen to make himself a beef sandwich.

Now that his manuscript had been safely dispatched to the publishers, he had more time to concentrate on the renovations to his home, and Arabella had been full of ideas, mostly impractical, with the earnest intention of doing things 'on the cheap'. He had never been more entertained in his life.

After lunch he wandered out into the garden. It was Saturday and he was at a loose end. Hearing footsteps on the drive, he glanced up in surprise.

'Good afternoon, Professor Fenner,' Emma said.

She was marching determinedly

towards him with her colour high and her red-gold hair swinging about her shoulders. Jeremy thought he had never seen a sight more magnificent.

'Miss Milton.'

'I'll get straight to the point' Emma informed him crisply, hiding her nervousness. 'I believe my brother spoke to you this morning about your need for some garden design. I have come to offer my services.'

At her defiant tone Jeremy almost smiled. 'How good of you.'

Somewhat encouraged, Emma held out her business card. 'I run Greenhills Garden Services and would be happy to give you a quotation for any work you require.' Her doe eyes challenged him to refuse.

Jeremy took the card and perused it carefully in order to hide his consternation. He was experiencing an unexpected rush of blood to the head which had left him feeling punch drunk.

Surely he wasn't attracted to her?

The woman was affecting him badly and it wasn't only because she had more curves than a barrow full of snakes, either. It was the whole package which was Emma Milton.

When he looked up his dark eyes were filled with questions, and some other, indefinable element he was unable to hide.

Seeing it, Emma caught her breath. She was flustered enough without this incredible man looking at her as though she had just made his day. 'Shall I come back another time?'

'No, now is fine,' Jeremy assured her in a casual voice.

There was a self-deprecating gleam of amusement in his eyes. What was happening here? He'd known far more glamorous women in his time and yet this appealing firebrand in her gardening boots and grubby jeans was turning him into a star-struck schoolboy.

Emma stood holding her breath, unaware of Jeremy's strong feelings. 'Where shall we start?' she prompted.

There was a sinking feeling in the pit of her stomach. He didn't look too impressed, and the truth was she was depending on this assignment, only she didn't want to appear too eager.

Jeremy made an effort to control his breathing. He'd never believed in love at first sight before, but he sure did now.

His intellect came to his rescue and informed him that any initial attraction to a woman was purely chemical. It would pass off in a minute or two, like a sudden fit of vertigo.

He cleared his throat. 'We'll start here and then go around the back, and you can tell me what you think.'

'Fine.'

Relieved, Emma gazed about her. 'For a start, there is an awful lot of sand around, isn't there?'

'What? Oh . . . that's Arabella's sand. I daresay I can clear it away before — '

'Did you say Arabella's sand?' Emma's tones were sharp. What did her sister have to do with anything?

'Well, yes. She and her friend, Peter, had some idea about covering my car with clods of earth a few weeks ago. Just a harmless bit of fun, but I'm afraid I've been too busy until now to clear it from the driveway.'

Emma swallowed, unable to believe what she was hearing. 'Are you saying that the children made all this mess?' she demanded. 'I thought . . . ' she trailed off, aghast to think that she'd railed at him about it, accusing him of unreasonable behaviour, when all the time it was her sister who had been at fault.

Gathering her courage, she looked him firmly in the eye.

'It seems I owe you an apology, Professor.' Her colour heightened. 'You had every reason to tell the children to clear off, and I attacked you like a shrew. I'm sorry.'

Jeremy observed the flush and fought a strong desire to take her into his arms and kiss her. 'No problem. Shall we continue? I'm not much of a gardener so you'll have to produce all the ideas.'

Emma recovered her poise and became business-like. She had plenty of ideas and some strong views about design, and became more and more enthusiastic as she visualised the potential, rattling on knowledgeably about pruning and patio plants and hardy annuals and spring bedding.

'As to layout, I suggest clearing this area and planting more lawn in order to give a more spacious feel, although there's lots of space already, I know. We could plant one or two shade trees like Tipana which is quick growing . . . and a water garden over here would be nice, don't you think, with some lovely pond plants and a little pump which runs your fountain . . . ?'

She beamed up at him, quite carried away. 'We'll have a wild bit beyond the lawn where indigenous bushes would blend naturally into the nearby veldt. It would encourage the bird life in your garden . . . but of course you would know all about that.'

Jeremy watched in fascination the lithe, graceful movements of her tanned, bare arms as she gestured. Her gazelle's eyes were alight with warmth and enthusiasm. Gone was the cagey little madam of a few moments ago.

Emma said suddenly, 'What a beautiful place you have, Professor Fenner.'

'Please call me Jeremy. Yes, I am very fortunate.'

'Oh, I couldn't possibly call you Jeremy, it wouldn't be very business-like, would it?'

She took a deep breath and continued, ' . . . all that wonderful veldt . . . what do you intend to do with it? The previous owner didn't do any farming, you know, just a few horses in one of the pastures.'

Jeremy was purposely vague. 'I have a few plans . . . '

'Just look at all that grassland in the distance,' Emma enthused, 'it's owned by some old man, I believe. It's a marvellous area, all of ten square miles, called Riverbush,' She chatted on, unaware that he knew every inch of the territory in question like the back of his hand. 'It's beautiful and wild, and I just wish the old codger would do something with it.'

She looked up, her golden-brown eyes intelligent and intense. Jeremy found that he couldn't look away. He asked carefully, 'Like what?'

'Well, it would make a wonderful nature reserve, wouldn't it? With a hutted camp, or even a game park. It needn't be the sort of tourist attraction which detracts from the wildness of the place, but somewhere where city people could experience the glories of nature and be at peace.'

Jeremy's breath caught in his throat. She could almost read his mind! 'Oh, quite,' he said casually, and changed the subject.

By the end of the half-hour he felt as though he'd discovered hidden treasure. Emma Milton was a very different kind of woman from what he'd imagined, and certainly no nutcase.

From the things she'd said he sensed an honesty and dignity about her, coupled with a sense of devotion to her family which endeared her further.

They had an extraordinary affinity. Did she feel it too? He hated to sound soppy, but it was as though they were soul mates, a term he'd never have dreamt of using before now.

There appeared to be a compatibility of a very strong and emotionally charged kind, and it was overwhelming. He had never felt this way about any woman before.

'I'll let you have a breakdown of the costs on Monday,' Emma told him, resuming her brisk manner. 'Should the quotation be satisfactory, I'd like to get started straight away.'

Jeremy found that he could hardly wait, either. Whatever figure she came up with was fine by him, he would commission the work anyway.

At least he'd be able to assess whether she really was the avaricious, man-mad gold-digger Craig had described. She certainly did not strike him as being desperate to find herself a man. In fact, she'd shown no inclination to attract him at all. Rather contrarily, he now found himself wishing that she had.

Emma was thoughtful as she walked home. It was unfortunate that Arabella's overworked imagination had misled her. She'd believed Jeremy Fenner was a complete ogre, but how wrong she'd been. It was a shock to find that his charm and magnetism both excited and disturbed her . . . not to mention those extraordinary good looks.

Over the past few years she'd been too involved with her work and too preoccupied with caring for her family to have had much time for a social life. To be frank, she lacked experience with men, so that when she met someone so intensely male and shatteringly attractive she was at a loss to know how to respond.

Should he commission her to do the work, she decided, she would just get on with the job and keep out of his way as much as she could. She would have to remind herself that Professor Jeremy Fenner was quite out of her league. All the same, she couldn't help wondering what it would be like to be loved by a man like that . . .

Her grandmother was sitting in the living-room with her knitting. She greeted Emma with a happy smile. 'I'm so pleased with my blue slippers, darling, they're comfortable enough for me to venture downstairs, so I have.'

'That's great, Gran.' At times like this, Emma felt that all her private financial battles were worthwhile.

'You're unusually flushed, dear.'

'Am I? Well, I've had a long walk.'

'So you have. Shall I make us some tea?'

'I'll make it, Gran.' Emma went into the kitchen to switch on the kettle. Arabella happened to be on the mat, playing with Fatcat's kittens. A basket had been brought into the kitchen to accommodate them.

'Arabella,' Emma challenged, 'you didn't tell me quite the truth about that sand, did you?'

Arabella looked blank. 'What sand?'

'I'm referring to the mess you and Peter made of Professor Fenner's driveway a few weeks ago. You led me to believe that he'd been unreasonable in chasing you away, when in fact he had every right to do so.'

'Oh, that.' Arabella stroked a kitten with one finger and sighed. 'I made a mistake, Emma. He's really a very nice man, even if that woman did die in his car. I asked him about it, you know.'

'Arabella, you didn't!'

'I did, and he said there'd been an accident. That's not the same as murdering someone, is it? I've decided not to call him Mr Monster any more. He's going to be Jolly Jeremy, instead.' She added blithely, 'We're great pals, you know. I'm helping him with his colours. I told him he must put in green carpets when he can afford them, not beige ones, because they would show the dirt.'

Emma gaped. 'Carpets? What are you talking about? Since when have you been to visiting Wozani to advise the professor about his carpets? Arabella, I fear you are becoming totally out of hand!'

'Well,' Arabella explained patiently, 'Peter and I sometimes have tea there on the way home from school, and we've discovered that he's not rich at all. In fact, he's very poor. He can't afford carpets in the house and there's hardly any furniture. He's really struggling, Emma.' She gave a huge sigh. 'I told him he should sell his car because it's not necessary to have such a big vehicle when there's only one of him.'

Emma felt the sudden need to sit down.

'Arabella, you didn't!' she repeated helplessly.

'I did. He just laughed and said he'd think about it, and it was very nice that I cared enough to advise him. Emma, you won't charge him a lot, will you?

For the gardening work, I mean. If you do, he'll probably starve himself to pay for it.'

Emma, a kind girl at heart, bit her lip. 'Oh, dear, I didn't know . . . no, I'll give him a very conservative estimate, don't worry.'

★ ★ ★

On Monday morning after Arabella had left for school and the kitchen had been tidied, Emma took herself down the hill in the Volvo. As promised, she was about to deliver a printed quotation to Jeremy's door.

Craig, fresh from a shower after his late lie-in, answered the doorbell. 'Good grief,' he said boldly, 'it's the redhead from Greenhills Farm. What on earth do you want with us?'

Emma greeted him politely and asked to see Professor Fenner.

Craig looked her up and down. 'I suppose you'd better come in.'

Emma stepped into the hall, glancing

covertly about her as she followed Craig into the large, sparsely furnished living-room. It was just as Arabella had said, the man was indeed poverty-stricken, and she was heartily glad she'd given him such generous terms.

Craig, scarcely able to contain his curiosity, went to fetch his cousin from the study and then stood listening unashamedly to the conversation.

'Should there be any difficulty with payment,' Emma concluded delicately, 'I'm prepared to discuss terms with you . . . it would not be a problem.'

Jeremy's face remained bland. 'How kind, but that will not be necessary. This quotation is perfectly in order, and I'd like you to begin as soon as possible.'

Emma's face lit in a brilliant smile, so that Jeremy blinked. 'Thank you.'

When she'd gone Craig gave a snigger.

'I didn't know you were such a skinflint, Jeremy. You allowed the girl to offer her services for a pittance, and what's more, she accepted. She needs her head examined! Do you know what you'd normally pay for all that work?' He quoted a figure which was well in excess of what Emma was asking.

Jeremy's tones were silky. 'I know what I'm doing, Craig.'

He returned to the study and closed the door so that Craig wouldn't see his shoulders shaking. He was well aware of what was happening here. Arabella had obviously informed her sister of his poverty-stricken state, and the girl, out of the goodness of her heart, had borne it in mind.

What Craig didn't know, of course, was that he had no intention of allowing Miss Milton to work for so little remuneration. Besides, her family obviously needed the money.

When the final cheque was due he would include a sizeable amount for 'customer satisfaction'.

It was wonderful, at last, to find a girl who wasn't a taker. If she were under the impression that he was a pauper, he would not enlighten her.

★　★　★

Antonia Miller was becoming bored with Craig Fenner. She flung her shoes across the room and reflected that more interesting by far was that exciting cousin of his, Jeremy. The man appeared to have money to burn, too.

Craig had told her he'd recently bought up five farms in the area, and on eliciting the name of his property broker, Antonia had made it her business to verify the details for herself.

She'd discovered a peculiar thing, each of the farms happened to border upon that vast area of grassland known as Riverbush.

Greenhills Farm, which Jeremy had enquired about, also adjoined Riverbush which reminded her of her clueless cousin, Emma.

'Greenhills,' she muttered mockingly, 'where Emma labours away night and day like a proper little worker bee. How boring can a woman get?'

Suddenly she sat upright and frowned. According to Craig, her cousin had recently inveigled herself into Jeremy's employ.

The hussy was now engaged in sorting out his garden, and according to Craig, Jeremy couldn't take his eyes off her!

It was time to take action. Emma must not be allowed to take what she, Antonia, wanted.

'Bring me a cup of tea, Maria,' Antonia yelled, summoning the surly housemaid from the kitchen.

When the tea duly arrived, she settled back to lay her plans. She would have Jeremy Fenner by means fair or foul, it made no difference, and in the process she'd show that gormless Emma just how a woman went about getting a man.

She studied the scrupulous notes she'd made on Jeremy, and spent a moment gloating over his assets. It was necessary to know as much as possible about a man's affairs when you intended to have him.

Her cat-like eyes glittered with satisfaction. Emma, she reflected smugly, didn't stand a chance. With men like Jeremy, who, it had to be said, was rather a gentleman, a woman had to take the initiative. She must find ways to make him notice her, like dazzling him with her intellect and competence, not to mention her beauty and her expensive designer clothes. No grubby gardening jeans and washed-out T-shirts for Antonia Milton!

A woman must demonstrate that she had her man's best interests at heart, Antonia decided. Efforts like acquiring Greenhills Farm for his property portfolio would impress.

After a few minutes, Antonia had worked out a strategy to her satisfaction. She went to her room to repair her make-up, snatched up her car keys and let herself out of the house.

★　★　★

Mrs Miller was enjoying the sunshine in the garden when Antonia arrived in her red BMW, complete with a large bouquet of roses she'd purchased at the florist's en route.

The old lady looked up in some surprise. 'Antonia! How lovely to see you, dear. You've not visited for some time.'

Antonia hid her annoyance. Did the old lady think she had nothing else to do other than dance attendance?

'I've been busy.' She thrust the bouquet at her grandmother and smiled insincerely. 'I thought I'd bring you some flowers, Gran. I don't suppose you get many these days.'

'On the contrary, dear, Emma always makes sure the vases are filled. But thank you, it's a lovely thought.'

Antonia scowled. Emma had always been Gran's favourite. Trust her to curry favour with the old lady by plying her with flowers! She should have brought chocolates instead.

She enquired sweetly, 'How are your feet, Gran?'

'Coming along nicely, dear. As you can see, I'm able to take a little walk into the garden now.'

'Ah, the garden.' Antonia looked around her and affected horrified surprise. 'Everything's become frightfully run down, hasn't it? It really isn't fair on Emma, you know.'

'What isn't, dear?'

Antonia allowed her disgust to show. 'Well, all this work. It's too much for her to cope with. Just look at the archway, it's practically falling over, and the white picket fence needs re-painting. I've never seen it all looking so run down. It's a disgrace.'

Mrs Milton paled. 'Run down? Too much for Emma? Do you really think so, dear?'

'I'm sure of it. Haven't you noticed how thin Emma's getting? Working too hard, I daresay.'

'Oh dear, perhaps you're right.'

'I have a suggestion, Gran. Why not sell the farm and move into one of those nice modern homes in Nelsburg, with a small garden to maintain and hardly any housework to do? It would be so much easier for you all, and much less bother for Emma.'

The old lady appeared to be shocked. 'Absolutely not! Greenhills is our home, Antonia. I shall never leave here. Besides, your cousins are happy enough.'

Concealing her irritation, Antonia begged the old lady to be reasonable. 'The land is not being utilised properly, and you know it. You could get quite a lot for it, you know.'

She added persuasively, 'I know someone who would buy it immediately. He's fabulously wealthy and you could virtually name your price. If you sold Greenhills you would have no more financial worries, you'd be rich, don't you see? It would ease the financial burden on Emma, who is obviously worried.'

'Even so, dear, we're not selling. Tom will farm the land again when the time comes. I have left Greenhills to him in my will.'

Antonia's mouth fell open. 'Surely my father should inherit when you die? He is your only surviving son, after all. It really isn't fair! Why leave it to a grandchild? And why Tom? There's me and Emma and Arabella too, you know.'

The old lady's eyes flashed. 'Your father is wealthy enough, Antonia, and you have your mother's money coming to you. No. You girls will have my jewellery and one or two small shares, but it is Tom who shall have the land, because he needs the start in life and will one day have to support a family of his own.' She added pointedly, 'I can trust him to look after his sisters when I'm gone.'

'But what does Tom know about farming? He'll ruin everything through mismanagement.'

'Well, he can learn, can't he? He's a sensible lad, and he helps Emma a lot in her business as it is.'

'Gran, I beg you to reconsider. If you sell the farm and buy a home in

Nelsburg there will be far more for Tom to inherit because the estate will be worth so much more . . . town property appreciates faster in value.'

She smiled encouragingly. 'I'll get the paperwork done for you and all you'll have to do is sign. I shall contact the client tomorrow, first thing. He's very wealthy, like I said, and he's very keen to have your land.'

But Mrs Milton was equally determined. 'It's kind of you to bother, dear, but my mind is quite made up.' She looked around a little desperately for Emma, who could always be relied upon to smooth things over. 'Would you like a cup of tea? Emma is around somewhere, and she'd be glad to give you a cup if you let her know you're here.'

Antonia went red with anger. 'No, I don't want tea,' she said shortly. 'I must say I think you're being obstinate and very, very foolish. See you, Gran.'

Mrs Milton sighed as she watched her granddaughter stalk away. Antonia was a most headstrong girl. Whatever had put such an idea into her head? Sell Greenhills indeed!

Antonia roared off in her car. The interview had not been a success, and it irked her considerably. She'd have to persuade her father to fall in with the next idea, and when Gran was more amenable, they would broker the deal together.

One way or another, she would present Jeremy Fenner with the land he wanted. Emma, of course, would be furious, which in fact filled Antonia with malicious satisfaction.

★ ★ ★

A few days later a letter arrived from Milton & Stanley, addressed to Mrs Victoria Milton. Seeing the letterhead, Gran surmised that it was a friendly communication from her son, Harris. She saw so little of him these days.

A moment later her face drained of colour.

'What is it, Gran?'

Wordlessly her grandmother handed her the letter. It was an offer to purchase Greenhills by a client of Milton & Stanley, who wished to remain anonymous.

I strongly advise you to consider this offer, Mother, Harris had written. *Antonia tells me that my late father's property is not being run properly and has become a liability to you. Furthermore, Emma herself recently informed me of your financial difficulties. Antonia will call on you to receive your signature. On hearing from you I shall proceed further . . . Yours, etc.*

Emma choked. 'How dare he! I spoke to him in confidence.'

Mrs Milton took out her handkerchief and wiped a tear from the corner of her eye. 'Is this true, Emma? You told Harris that we were in difficulties? I had no idea . . . '

Hiding her anger, Emma placed an arm about her grandmother's shoulders and decided to play things down a little. 'Yes, Gran,' she said gently, 'I did approach him because I wanted a . . . a business loan so I can expand the garden business, that's all. I thought it would help.' She added bleakly. 'He refused.'

'I see.' Mrs Milton sniffed. 'Harris was never generous, so I cannot say I'm surprised. Our situation is not serious, then?'

Emma crossed her fingers behind her back. 'There is no need to upset yourself, Gran,' she soothed, 'we've always managed in the past and we'll continue to manage in the future.'

'If you say so, dear. I just feel so awful about it all. You've not had any new clothes for ages.'

Emma kissed her cheek. 'What do I need clothes for? I'd spoil them in the garden. Everything will be all right, Gran. I have this new work for Professor Fenner, remember? He has promised to pay me weekly, too.'

'Then you don't think we should sell?'

'Absolutely not, if you don't want to. Greenhills is your home and Tom's heritage. We'll manage, don't worry.'

Her grandmother gave a watery smile. 'That's all right, then. I'll phone Harris in the morning.'

The decision, relayed to Milton & Stanley, sent Antonia into a fury.

'The old mule! She doesn't know what's good for her, does she, Daddy? It's ridiculous. We're only trying to help.'

Harris shrugged. 'Be it on Mother's own head. You came up with a brilliant idea as usual, my dear, which would have solved all their financial problems, but my mother will not listen. There is nothing more to be done.'

'Oh, but surely we can do something, Daddy?' Antonia's anger was replaced by an expression of concern. 'We can't allow them to live like paupers. Besides, Jeremy Fenner is an important client and he wants that land badly. We wouldn't want to disappoint him.'

'No, but I don't see what else we can do.'

Antonia did. She waited until her father was closeted in the boardroom with his partner, Ron Stanley, before using the telephone on his desk.

'Hello darling, how about taking me out to lunch?' she gushed. 'I have something interesting to discuss with you.'

Craig Fenner, having just surfaced from his bed, gave a great yawn. 'Like what?'

'Oh, I have one or two little jobs for you to undertake. All frightfully hush-hush, if you get me, but all in a good cause. I'll make it well worth your while, don't worry.'

Craig was intrigued. 'You mean you'll pay me? What sort of jobs?'

'Just meet me at one and I'll tell you. We'll eat at the Hazelton Hotel in Main Street, they have a superb new carvery.'

Antonia smirked as she replaced the receiver. She could read Craig Fenner like a book. He was a young man who would do anything for money, which suited her just fine. It would cost her a few thousand rands out of her savings, but what was a few thousand when so much was at stake?

6

'So what's it all about?' Craig demanded after sitting for fifteen minutes patiently waiting.

Antonia finished her soup and daintily touched her lips with her napkin. 'That's my secret,' she snapped.

'OK, keep your hair on! Keep your secrets, too, but if you want to involve me, I must know a certain amount,' he said firmly.

'You will be told what to do and when to do it, and that's all you need to know.'

'Knowing you, Antonia, I am forced to enquire if the jobs are to be entirely above board?'

'Oh, the ends justify the means, don't worry.'

'So when do I start?'

'Soon. I must stress it's top secret. You are to tell no-one, do you understand? I intend to make it so uncomfortable for them that the family is forced to leave Greenhills . . . all in their own best interests, naturally. Here's what I want you to do . . . '

When she'd finished, Craig stared at her in amazement. 'You're prepared to go to all those lengths just to get your grandmother to change her mind about selling? But why?'

'My reasons,' Antonia snapped, 'are my own. Well? Will you play?'

Craig looked thoughtful. 'There's just one thing. I'd like a written contract from you before I agree to do anything.'

'Don't be ridiculous, Craig. Why would you want a written contract?'

'Simple. I always hedge my bets. It will save my skin if anything goes wrong. How do I know you won't renege on payment?'

'You have my word.'

'All the same, those are my terms.' Craig folded his arms across his chest and told her implacably, 'Take it or leave it.'

Antonia sighed. 'Oh, all right, I'll do as you say. I'll not put in all the details, just the general idea, and the amount I'll pay you. Will that do?'

Craig grinned. 'Fine. Count me in.'

★　★　★

Emma hauled her gardening implements from the boot of the Volvo. She intended to start by removing Arabella's unsightly mess from the professor's driveway.

'Good morning, Miss Milton,' Jeremy greeted her. 'I'm glad to see you're on time. Where would you like to begin?'

'I thought I'd . . . ' her eyes widened. 'That soil . . . it's been cleared!'

'I had nothing to do yesterday afternoon so I thought I'd save you the trouble.' Why allow the girl to labour away when he could do it in half the time?

Emma blushed. 'But . . . you're paying me to do that.'

He looked severe. 'So? It's my

garden. I'm entitled to take a little exercise if I so wish.'

Her flush deepened. 'Oh, of course. I didn't mean . . . what I meant was, thank you very much.'

His veiled glance took in the shabby jeans, deplorable pink T-shirt and well-worn trainers. She looked like something the cat had brought in, and far too slender to engage in heavy manual work, at that. Surely she didn't intend to undertake the whole lot on her own?

He asked carefully, 'Does anyone help you in the business?'

Emma smiled brightly. 'Oh, yes, there's my brother, Tom, but he's rather taken up with schoolwork at the moment.'

Jeremy nodded. It was as he'd thought.

He said smoothly, 'Then you won't mind if I try my hand at a few things? I've a lot to learn when it comes to gardening.' He smiled encouragingly, 'I'd be grateful if you'd explain things to me as we go along.'

Emma gave a secret sigh of relief. It would be good to have his help.

Emma made a show of pulling on her gardening gloves. As she surveyed the shocking neglect around her the light of battle appeared in her golden eyes and a familiar rush of anticipation made itself felt in the pit of her stomach. This is what she loved most in all the world — creating beauty out of chaos!

'We'll start with the borders, shall we?' she told Jeremy briskly, adding encouragingly, 'you won't know them when we're finished. I've brought quite a lot of plants with me, mostly shrubs, and also some seedlings for immediate summer colour; they're in the back of the car. I'll explain later about how I mix colours and texture.'

Jeremy found her enthusiasm endearing. He was beginning to enjoy himself hugely. He'd never gardened in his life, but at that moment he would have tamed a jungle for her, no problem.

'I'm yours to command,' he smiled, feeling more light-hearted than he had in months.

Emma looked up into his dark eyes and her heart turned over. To cover her confusion she blurted, 'Good, because I'm about to teach you, Professor, what hard work is all about!'

At mid morning Craig sauntered out into the garden, having roused himself from sleep.

'Good heavens, Jeremy, since when have you joined Miss Milton to become the hired help?' he mocked.

Jeremy, who was not a violent man, felt like punching him. 'I would remind you that this is my garden and my time,' he said. 'If you've nothing else to do, Craig, you can make us a mug of coffee. And kindly remember your manners. Miss Milton is not the hired help, as you so unfortunately put it, she has been professionally commissioned by me to undertake work I am not competent to do myself.'

Craig looked thunderous. 'So sorry!'

he muttered sarcastically and returned to the house.

'I apologise for my cousin's rudeness,' Jeremy said tightly.

Emma smiled. 'We both appear to have . . . cousin difficulties.'

'Meaning?'

'Well . . . Antonia Milton, my cousin . . . I believe I saw you at her father's chambers recently. For some reason she'd like to consign me to the crocodiles, and I have never quite been able to discover why. It doesn't much bother me, but I wish she'd be more civil to our grandmother.'

The moment she had divulged this, Emma could have bitten her tongue out. She hadn't intended to blurt out her private irritations, it wasn't very professional. It was just that Jeremy Fenner was that kind of man — understanding, kind, compassionate. He made one feel safe.

At lunch-time she called a halt. The sun was hot, and despite the coffee Craig had supplied, she was once more dying of thirst.

'I have to give my grandmother her meal, I'll be back in an hour's time,' she promised, dabbing at her forehead with a handkerchief. In the process she left a muddy smudge down her cheek. Jeremy found it most endearing.

'Thank you very much for the help, Professor.'

'Please call me Jeremy.'

Emma felt suddenly shy. Professor Fenner was an attractive man and she must try to remember to keep him at a suitable distance. He was, after all, a business client.

It was as though Jeremy had read her thoughts. 'We're neighbours as well, you know,' he pointed out blandly.

Jeremy opened the car door for her. 'I don't bite,' he added in a mild voice, 'and I'm fully house-trained. See you later, Emma.'

Mrs Milton appeared to be a little flustered when Emma entered the living-room.

'What is it, Gran?'

'Antonia was here again, trying to get me to sell, and I said no. The dear girl can be so tiresome!' She regarded Emma uncertainly. 'Do you think I'm doing the right thing, Emma?'

'Yes, Gran, I do. However, it's your property, so it must be your decision.'

'I know. It's just that I came here as a bride and it would be such a wrench to have to leave now.'

'Of course it would, and nobody is forcing you out. Now, how about an omelette and salad for your lunch?'

'Lovely, dear. Tell me, how is the work going at Professor Fenner's? Arabella tells me he is a most charming man, but struggling to make ends meet, I believe. Perhaps you would take him one of my jars of marmalade? There are three left in the pantry.'

★　★　★

At ten minutes to two Emma drove back down the hill and surveyed the morning's work. Thanks to all the help

Jeremy had given her the borders were now fully prepared, having been suitably weeded and dug over with compost. She was positioning the various plants and shrubs in their little black bags ready for planting when Jeremy appeared and was duly presented with Mrs Milton's marmalade.

He looked surprised. 'How kind. Please thank your grandmother. Nobody has ever given me home-made marmalade before.'

Emma smiled. He appeared to be genuinely touched, and her kind heart melted. 'Wait until you taste her peach preserve. She's not much of a cook generally, but she's not bad when it comes to bottling fruit. I make quite a mean peach tart using two jars, with lashings of whipped cream. Perhaps you'd like to come to dinner one evening and try it? At least you'd be getting a good square meal . . . ' she clapped her hand over her mouth. What had made her make such an insensitive remark?

Jeremy appeared not to have noticed. 'I'd be delighted,' he assured her gravely, hiding his laughter.

Emma did a hasty calculation. A pork chop and apricot casserole, perhaps?

'Would Saturday evening suit you, then? Sevenish.'

'That's very kind. Saturday it is.' Jeremy picked up the spade. 'I'll dig the holes for this lot, shall I? As I'm quite incapable of singing for my supper, I shall dig for it instead.'

By the end of the afternoon she found herself wholeheartedly agreeing with Arabella. Jeremy Fenner was the most wonderful man in the world.

Arabella, at that moment toiling up the hill from the bus stop, was nursing her latest secret. It was the strong desire that Jolly Jeremy would fall in love with her sister, Emma.

She stopped in surprise. Why was their Volvo parked in Jeremy's drive? It was then that she remembered that Emma was now employed at Wozani. With an excited yelp she hitched her schoolbag over her shoulder and ran towards the house.

On seeing Jeremy she hurled herself at him with a delighted smile. 'Hello, Jolly Jeremy, are you helping my sister in the garden?'

Jeremy took her schoolbag from her and clapped her on the shoulder. 'Hello Arabella. Actually, your sister's helping me, and I'm most grateful. How does it look?'

Arabella glanced about without much interest. 'Fine. Where's Emma?'

'Gone to turn on the tap so we can hose these plants. Want to help?'

'Oh, I'm sorry but I must go home and write my story for Mrs Fletcher. It's about giants this time.'

Arabella's expression became stern. 'Jolly Jeremy,' she advised, 'it's time you started looking for someone to marry.'

Jeremy's eyes gleamed. 'Oh, is that so?'

'Emma would do,' she hinted broadly. 'She's not so bad when you get used to her, and she makes humongous muffins. You'll never go hungry.'

★ ★ ★

By Friday, Emma had completed the borders, mown the extensive lawns around the house and begun digging the foundation for Jeremy's water garden.

'Here. Let me do that,' he told her, hurrying outside after noting her labours from the study window.

Emma tossed her mane of hair over one shoulder. 'Oh, I can manage.'

'Of course you can.' Jeremy sounded as though he were pacifying a small child, 'but I can do it much faster, and besides, I need you to go and pour us some orange juice.'

Secretly relieved, Emma did as she was told. She was by now familiar with the layout of his kitchen, and knew where to find the glasses. She opened the refrigerator and was shocked to note how extremely meagre the contents were.

'Poor man, I'll make sure he has a decent meal tomorrow evening,' she murmured, quite unaware that Craig had been prevailed upon to empty the appliance for cleaning only that morning, prior to being substantially restocked.

She took the tray outside and handed Jeremy a tall glass of orange juice.

He smiled. 'Thanks, Ginger.'

Emma gave him a fierce look. 'My hair is not ginger, it's auburn.'

Jeremy slapped his forehead. 'My mistake. May I atone for the oversight and say how pretty it is?'

Emma went scarlet. 'You may, but I'd much rather you kept your mind on your work, Professor. I want this pond cemented by sunset.'

'Yes, ma'am.' He touched his forelock mockingly. 'It shall be done just as you say, ma'am.'

'I shan't be working for you tomorrow, as it's Saturday,' Emma thought to inform him a moment later.

Jeremy quelled his disappointment. 'Oh, of course.'

Emma darted him a glance from under her eyelashes. 'I'll be too busy cooking up a storm . . . you're coming to dinner, remember?'

He brightened. 'So I am. I'll bring the wine.'

She looked suddenly worried. 'Oh, but there's no need . . . wine can be expensive . . . I mean . . . ' she peeped at him again, 'oh dear, I'm afraid I've offended you.'

Deliberately Jeremy reached for her glass and deposited it, together with his own, on the tray.

'No, you haven't. On the contrary, it is nice to have someone so concerned for my welfare.'

He drew her close, bent his head and kissed her soft, pink mouth.

Emma's response was instinctive. She kissed him back, and felt the earth move beneath her feet.

'Oh, that was very nice,' she gasped.

'Would you do it again?' The words were out before she could stop them, and she wanted to disappear in a cloud of smoke.

Jeremy, needing no encouragement, hastened to oblige. He kissed her thoroughly and felt a tide of love well up inside him. It was overwhelming.

Emma, caught close against the solid muscles of his chest, felt the racing of Jeremy's heartbeat and knew without doubt that this was the man she'd been waiting for. She stared up at him in bemusement, quite unable to utter a word.

Jeremy cleared his throat. 'Er . . . as pleasant as that interlude was, we have a job to do. Shall we get on?'

Emma nodded, still at a loss for words. She had fallen headlong in love with this most wonderful man and there was nothing at all she could do about it. She hugged her secret to herself and decided sadly, as she drove home, that she had been a very foolish girl. One or two kisses meant nothing to an experienced man like Jeremy, who was quite out of her league. Which sentiment didn't stop her from loving him even more.

★ ★ ★

It was the following morning when Tom went outside to water the plants that he discovered the carnage. All the tomato plants which he and Emma had tended so lovingly, were ripped from their beds and strewn around the floor of the greenhouse, as were the trays of annuals and lettuce seedlings. Most of them had been ruthlessly trampled, smashed beyond recognition. Bags of compost had been emptied all over the floor, mixed with fragments of glass from the shattered panes of the greenhouse walls.

Quickly he checked the other greenhouse. It appeared to have suffered an even worse fate. 'Emma!' he yelled, and ran to find her.

Emma, having just discovered her

own scene of destruction in the front garden, was looking furious. 'Someone's hacked down all our shrubs during the night, and cut the fence wire in three places!' she stormed.

'They've been busy in the greenhouses, too. Come and see.'

Wordlessly Emma followed him around the side of the house. As they neared the chicken run they discovered that the door had been removed from its hinges, all the eggs smashed and one or two birds lying with their necks wrung. The rest, twenty-five in all, had disappeared into the veld.

'What the blazes is going on?' Emma demanded. 'Who would do a thing like this? We have no enemies that I know of. It's an utter nightmare!'

It took them the whole morning to fix things as best they could, but the fact remained there would be no plants to sell and no vegetables for the supermarket. Even the potato plants had been pulled up from their beds behind the barn, beds which had been so carefully weeded by Tom the previous week.

'The chickens will be eaten within days by the lynxes and civet cats,' Emma sighed. They were Gran's pride and joy, and she would be heartbroken. Besides, they had come to rely on the small income from the sale of the eggs.

By the time Emma took herself inside to begin the evening meal she was in no mood for a jolly evening. Arabella sat stroking one of the kittens, her eyes huge. 'Do you think they'll come back and do any more damage?' she asked fearfully.

'I shouldn't think so, darling,' Emma said, more confidently than she felt.

'We'll have nothing to sell now. No lettuces or tomatoes.'

'No. We'll just have to plant some more, and then work harder to recoup our losses.'

Emma smiled brightly. 'Would you like to make us a small posy for the table tonight? Use some of those pink daisies from the bush by the front door, it's the only one which wasn't hacked to bits.'

'Shouldn't we tell the police we've been vandalised?' Arabella asked.

'Tom will phone them on Monday morning, but there's very little they can do about it now. We'll just have to be more vigilant, I suppose. The dogs could sleep outside in the barn in future.'

Emma tied on her apron. 'Now, let's forget all about this nonsense,' she suggested, 'and when you've done the flowers you can offer to have a game of cards with Gran, she could do with some cheering up. And Arabella . . . '

'Yes, Emma?'

'You are not to breath a word about our troubles to anyone, do you hear? It is our business, and ours alone.'

'Yes, Emma.'

Despite the misfortunes of the day, the evening turned out to be a pleasant one. Jeremy arrived on time, armed with two bottles of expensive wine and a box of chocolates for Gran, who decided after a few minutes that he was the nicest young man she had met in ages.

Jeremy did full justice to the meal Emma had prepared and expressed his appreciation suitably as he rose to leave a few hours later.

'That peach tart was something else,' he enthused as Emma saw him to the car, 'thank you once again, Emma. It is some time since I enjoyed such a wonderful, home-cooked meal.'

'A pleasure,' she murmured politely, taking a step backwards. She hadn't forgotten his kisses and her spontaneous response to them, and was determined it would not happen again. She would be better off playing it cool or she'd find herself in deeper water than she cared to.

'I'll see you on Monday, as usual. We'll line the water garden and fill it before putting in the waterside plants. Goodbye, Jeremy.'

Sensing her sudden reserve, Jeremy simply nodded. 'See you, Emma.'

Craig was walking through the hall with a mug of coffee, having just reported to Antonia the success of his previous evening's undertakings. He looked up as Jeremy came into the house and asked innocently, 'How was your evening?'

Jeremy hung his jacket on the peg. 'Very pleasant.'

'Is that all you can say?'

'What else would you have me say?'

'Well, were there any problems? I mean, did anyone complain of anything?'

Jeremy's eyes narrowed. 'Just what are you getting at, Craig?'

'I heard there were a few problems at Greenhills this morning . . . just something someone said in town. Er, nothing was said . . . ?'

'No.'

Craig took himself into his bedroom, shut the door and sat down on the bed to think. It was amazing that the Miltons had said nothing about their misfortunes. He almost felt cheated.

Not that the convoluted workings of Antonia's mind were any of his business, he told himself with a shrug. He was just there to earn a bit on the side. He'd successfully completed the first part, and the next job would have to be executed tonight. Then he could demand his cheque. It might be as well not to stick around too much longer in Nelsburg, in case there were unpleasant repercussions.

Craig looked at his watch and yawned. There was still plenty of time and he would fill it by studying his racing form books. With luck Jeremy wouldn't awaken when he crept out in the early hours. He'd purposely parked his car outside the gate for a quick, quiet getaway . . .

7

At nine o'clock on Sunday morning, Arabella wandered forlornly down the hill, discussing their latest catastrophe with her friend, Peter Mazibuko.

'Gran is very upset,' she informed him in a subdued little voice, 'I saw her crying.'

Jeremy, with an hour to spare before driving into Nelsburg for the church service, had decided to inspect the fences near the road with the intention of asking Emma's advice about planting a few hedges.

'Hello, kids.' He smiled. 'I thought you'd be at Sunday School by now.'

'Oh, we're not going to church today,' Arabella told him sadly, 'we've had a . . . a misfortune.' She gazed at him with tragic, red-rimmed eyes.

'Oh dear, you've been crying. Would you like to tell me all about it?'

All at once she released the sobs she'd been withholding on account of not wanting to cry in front of Peter.

'Awful things have been h-happening, but I'm not . . . not allowed to talk about it.' She gulped. 'Goodbye.' She turned and rushed back up the hill.

Jeremy rubbed his chin thoughtfully. They had both looked most unhappy. Realising it was not strictly his business, he nevertheless went inside to fetch his car keys. If something had occurred to upset the family who had been kind enough to give him that wonderful meal last night, the least he could do was offer to help in some way. The truth was, he couldn't bear to think that Emma was in any kind of trouble.

As he turned into the entrance to Greenhills Farm an acrid smell reached his nostrils as clouds of black smoke belched out from behind the homestead. He parked hurriedly in the forecourt and raced around the side of the house.

The barn, or what was left of it,

together with the adjacent outbuildings, had been reduced to a smouldering ruin. Emma and Tom, having brought the blaze under control in the early hours of the morning by means of the hose pipes which were used to irrigate the vegetables, were standing beside their grandmother with miserable, blackened faces.

'Oh, it's you,' Emma said when she saw him, and only just prevented herself from rushing into his arms. Instead, she burst into angry tears.

Mrs Milton, still in her dressing gown and slippers, greeted Jeremy tremulously. 'Isn't it dreadful?' she quavered, wiping her eye with the corner of a handkerchief.

Jeremy looked around him in consternation, oddly at a loss. There was nothing much he could say.

'You've done a good job in containing it,' he conceded at length.

Emma's voice was low and furious. 'I can't believe this has happened to us. All our seeds and implements are ruined, the wooden handles burned to cinders . . . everything we've worked so hard for . . . '

She gulped. 'Even the lawn mowers were ruined when the petrol exploded. All I can say is, thank goodness the cats were in a basket in the kitchen, and the dogs were upstairs.'

'If there'd been a strong wind the house would have caught fire too,' Tom added.

'Any idea what caused it?' Jeremy asked.

Tom gave him a strange, half apprehensive look. 'Don't ask.'

'It was arson,' Emma blurted. 'What else, coming on top of yesterday's carnage? Someone is trying to ruin us.'

Jeremy remembered Craig's unusual questions on the previous evening and his brows came down sharply into a scowl. Had Craig known more than he'd been prepared to say?

'Please explain,' he ordered tersely.

So Tom did. 'You see,' he finished, 'it does rather look as though we've one or two enemies. Trouble is, who?'

Mrs Milton sniffed. 'Perhaps we should move into town, after all. It pains me to say it but Antonia is right. She was quite adamant about it and I daresay it makes sense . . . I ought to sell Greenhills. We really can't keep on like this.'

Her lips quivered. 'I've been a selfish old woman, allowing you children to work night and day just so that my wishes could be indulged, and now you'll have to work even harder to recoup the losses we've sustained . . . ' She took a moment to compose herself and added, 'I cannot allow it. I shall telephone Antonia at once before I change my mind. She said she knows someone who wants to buy the land.'

'Grandmother, please!' Emma begged.

'Let's go inside for some breakfast,' Tom said quickly. 'Don't do anything in a hurry, Gran.' He took her arm. 'I'll make you a nice cup of tea and you'll soon feel better. Come along, love, let me help you into the house.'

Jeremy looked at Emma. He said slowly, 'Let me get this straight. Your cousin, Antonia, has been pressurising your grandmother to sell Greenhills Farm?'

'Yes, she's been rather insistent, as a matter of fact. She has a buyer who has been enquiring about our land and apparently he's very wealthy. She says we can name our price — not that we're really interested.'

Jeremy's jaw hardened. 'I see!'

'Antonia is a very determined person,' Emma explained. 'Unfortunately she's the kind of person who will stop at nothing to get what she wants.' Her eyes widened in sudden incredulity. 'You don't think . . . you don't think Antonia has anything to do with the fire? Surely she wouldn't . . . surely not . . . ' she finished helplessly.

Jeremy bent and kissed her gently on the cheek. 'That,' he said grimly, 'is what I intend to find out.'

★ ★ ★

On Monday morning Jeremy drove into Nelsburg and parked outside the offices of Milton & Stanley, Solicitors.

'I have an appointment with Harris Milton,' he informed the receptionist briskly.

'Certainly sir, you are expected. Come this way.'

The solicitor rose from his desk with an expansive greeting. 'Good morning, Professor Fenner, it's a fine day, is it not? How may I help you?' He waved a hand. 'You remember my daughter, Antonia? She was present at our last interview.'

He nodded in her direction. 'Miss Milton.'

Antonia smiled sweetly. 'Do be seated, Jeremy. How simply lovely to see you again, and please call me Antonia. Would you like a cup of coffee?'

Equally politely Jeremy declined. This was not a social visit. 'I'll get straight to the point,' he said firmly. 'It concerns the land owned by Mrs Victoria Milton.

The farm known as Greenhills. I believe I mentioned it on my previous visit.'

'Yes, yes, I remember,' Harris assured him impatiently, 'my mother had been approached.'

' . . . And is considering the matter,' Antonia interrupted hastily. 'I'm quite sure that we will have some good news for you in a very short space of time.'

She shot Jeremy a guileless look from beneath her false eye lashes and confided, 'you know what old people are, they need a little time.'

'And inducement.'

'I beg your pardon?'

'Old people,' Jeremy said clearly, 'need to be given enough reason to comply with one's request. In short, they sometimes need coercion.'

Antonia looked smug. 'Oh, too right.'

'In that case, perhaps you will not mind describing the type of coercion you used?' Jeremy suggested silkily. 'I would be most interested to hear your methods.'

Antonia's smile broadened. 'Shall we

just say, I've been rather ingenious? Oh, I'm not saying I applied any more pressure than was reasonable.'

'No.' Jeremy agreed pleasantly, 'you simply employed another to do so for you.'

Harris looked sharply from one to the other. 'What's all this? What are you implying, Fenner?'

'Your daughter,' Jeremy told him, his eyes as hard as steel, 'has been using some rather unorthodox methods to make your mother agree to letting me have her land.'

'Oh? Is that so, Antonia?' Harris gave her an indulgent glance. 'You've made my mother see sense at last, have you?'

He beamed. 'I always said you were quite brilliant. Er, what methods?'

'Unpleasant ones,' Jeremy said clearly.

Antonia began to look sulky. 'I have no idea what you mean, Jeremy.'

'Yes, you do. You hired my cousin, Craig, to vandalise your grandmother's property, did you not? An undertaking for which you paid him this morning a very considerable sum. In cash.'

Antonia swallowed. 'What nonsense!' Remembering that she was about to become a lawyer, she drew herself up haughtily. 'You can't prove a thing.'

Jeremy pulled a piece of paper from his inside pocket. 'I have here the written agreement you so foolishly gave my cousin a few days ago. I found it in his shirt pocket when I was doing the laundry this morning. I've had a long talk with Craig, who had readily admitted his culpability, after which he decided to pack his bags and leave for Cape Town.

'I allowed him to do so on the condition that he be prepared to return and testify against you in court when you are charged with arson. Not to mention sundry other unsavoury activities.'

Antonia was staring at him in shock. 'I . . . I . . . '

'Rubbish!' her father exploded. 'I will not have my daughter maligned in this fashion, young man. You would be advised to watch your mouth. Wild accusations of this nature could land you in trouble.'

'If you weren't so besotted a parent, Milton, you'd be the first to see that I'm speaking the truth. Your daughter has behaved abominably. What she has been responsible for perpetrating in the last two days has been nothing short of criminal. Perhaps you should ask her about it.'

For a moment Harris looked uncertain. 'Antonia . . . ?'

'I only did it for him,' she whined, casting Jeremy a reproachful look. 'You should be pleased that I went to so much trouble on your behalf, Professor Fenner.'

'What trouble?' her father demanded.

She turned beseeching eyes on him. 'Oh, one or two little things, Daddy. I was only trying to help. I never intended any harm.'

'Of course you didn't,' Harris agreed rapidly. He rose. 'Now that you have made your unpleasant accusations, Fenner, I would ask you to leave. I have other more important things to do with my time than listen to your drivel.'

Jeremy's tones were coldly civil. 'Not so fast. I have something else to say to you, Milton.'

'If it's anything to do with Greenhills,' Harris said pompously, 'allow me to point out that I am a man of my word and am therefore still prepared to broker the deal as soon as my mother agrees to the sale, as Antonia had indicated that she will do shortly. After that, Fenner, I must ask you to find yourself another solicitor.'

'Oh, I intend to,' Jeremy assured him pleasantly. 'However, with regard to Greenhills, I will not be requiring your services. Hereafter I intend to negotiate personally with Mrs Victoria Milton.'

'In which case I shall find ways and means to render the sale null and void,' Harris snapped peevishly. 'You will not be allowed to play fast and loose with my family!'

'If you interfere in my affairs any way whatsoever,' Jeremy grated, 'I shall bring certain charges against you which are long overdue.'

Harris laughed. 'For what?'

'For fraudulently endeavouring to obtain the title deeds to the property known locally as Riverbush.'

Harris stared at him in shock. 'I don't know what you mean,' he blustered.

'Oh, I think you do, but if necessary I will jog your memory. You will recall that my late uncle, a certain Doctor James Henry Willis-Green, was a client of yours. He died a few weeks ago.'

'So?'

'He visited you two days before his death in order to finalise his estate, and on that occasion you agreed to prepare his last will and testament. You were therefore party to the fact that a nephew was to inherit the land known as Riverbush.'

The solicitor glared back defiantly. 'What are you getting at?'

'Just this. Before my uncle could put

his signature to the papers you'd prepared, he died. You then changed the will, substituting your name for the nephew's in order to make yourself the beneficiary of the land in question.'

'That's preposterous!'

'Is it? I have reason to believe that you intend presenting the unsigned will to the executors for probate in the hope that you will shortly be granted the title deeds to the property.

'For this purpose you have recently approached a Durban architect to draw up plans for an upmarket resort which you intend to develop there.'

Harris went pale. 'I advise you to be very careful, Fenner. I could sue you for slander. You cannot prove any of this.'

'The architect in question,' Jeremy went on relentlessly, 'telephoned me immediately. He is a close, and trusted, friend of mine. He had indicated he would be willing to testify to this in a court of law.

'So you see, Milton, you can't keep your dirty secret and get away with it.'

His jaw tightened. 'Furthermore, I am Doctor Willis-Green's nephew. I have always known that Riverbush would be mine, and therefore set about making a thorough search for any possible second will my uncle may have left. I was unsuccessful until last week, when I was unpacking the box of books he'd left me.'

He pulled an envelope from his pocket. 'I discovered this hand-written will, signed, dated and witnessed by his housekeeper and her daughter. It was made before my uncle even consulted you and states than I am the rightful beneficiary. Need I say any more?'

Harris looked suddenly very old. 'All right,' he admitted heavily, 'What you say is true. I was greedy.' He was unable to hide his sudden apprehension. 'You'll not take this further? I could be struck off . . .'

'So you could.'

'What . . . what would you have me do?'

'You will destroy the so-called will

156

you altered, and lay no claim whatsoever to the land in question. I shall instruct the solicitor who has always acted for me — John Morley of Morley & Hallowes in Durban — to present the handwritten will for probate. Thereafter, as far as I'm concerned, Milton, this conversation never happened.'

Harris looked astounded. 'That's . . . decent of you,' he mumbled. 'Why?'

Jeremy pocketed the envelope. 'Because,' he said coldly, 'like my late uncle, I detest publicity. I will not have my life disrupted by newshounds sniffing around my front door like a pack of wolves.'

He paused. 'Secondly, as we are to be related in the near future, we must make an effort to be reasonably congenial, must we not? If only for the sake of my future wife.'

Harris's jaw fell open. 'Related?'

'That's correct. I intend to ask your niece, Emma Milton to marry me.'

Jeremy strode to the door. 'Good day, Milton . . . Antonia. I can't say it's been a pleasure. I shall see myself out.'

Harris sat up for a full twenty seconds with his jaw still hanging open. Aroused at last by an unpleasant noise which had penetrated his numbed brain, he turned around to see what it was.

It was Antonia, sobbing furiously in the corner.

8

As soon as Antonia had composed herself sufficiently, she went to the ladies' rest room, slammed the door and pulled out her mobile telephone.

That wretch, Emma! How could Jeremy do this to her, especially after she'd been to so much trouble on his behalf? She'd show them! What Jeremy didn't know was that she still had one more ace up her sleeve.

'Emma, is that you?' she asked in a sugary voice. 'Darling, I've just heard about it, the fire. I'm so sorry.'

Emma's greeting was guarded. She was just about to return to Wozani after having come home to prepare her grandmother's lunch and did not wish to be late. 'Oh, hello Antonia. Do you want to speak to Gran?'

'No, it's you I'm after. I have some news for you.'

'Oh? Well, be quick, I only have a few minutes.'

'Sure.'

Antonia smiled nastily to herself. 'Craig Fenner has just telephoned me to say that his cousin, Jeremy, is to blame for all your troubles. You see, he's been after your land all along, and that's what he came to consult Daddy about that day you saw him in our building.

'Naturally we told him to get lost, but he's a very persistent man. Craig says he's been determined to hound you all out of Greenhills.'

Emma went white. 'Are you sure?'

'Positive. Why would Craig lie? Jeremy's a bad lot and my advice is to stay away from the man. Just thought I'd tip you off . . . '

She rang off and gave a spiteful laugh.

There wouldn't be any weddings on the horizon now!

Emma went to her room and sat on the bed, shaking with fury. Her stomach felt half churned to death. To think that she had fallen in love with an utter pig like Jeremy Fenner!

She couldn't wait to confront the hypocritical jerk, and then she'd go straight to the Nelsburg police station and have him charged.

With deliberation Emma took a shower and changed her clothes. Partly to bolster her confidence and partly due to some perverse feminine whim, she put on her smartest outfit, a sleeveless sheath and matching jacket which echoed the fiery tones of her hair.

Satisfied that her make-up was perfect, she brushed her glossy head one more time before spraying herself liberally with perfume and went to find her grandmother.

'Gran, I'll not be working for Professor Fenner as usual this afternoon. I have an appointment in Nelsburg, but I'll be back in time to give you your afternoon tea.'

Mrs Milton looked up from her knitting. 'All right, dear.'

She surveyed her granddaughter proudly. 'You look as pretty as a flame lily, Emma. I love the copper-coloured shoes and matching belt. Some young man,' she added playfully, 'will snap you up one of these days.'

★　★　★

Jeremy's Mercedes, she noted in relief when she reached Wozani, was parked in the garage, which meant he'd returned from town. He'd been out all morning, leaving her to get on with the garden.

With her hair flaming behind her, Emma marched to the front door and rang the bell.

'Hello, Emma,' Jeremy said, and did a double-take. 'You look stunning! No gardening for you this afternoon, I take it?'

'You take it correctly, Professor,' she replied icily. 'No gardening ever again, mister. I quit!'

His gaze never faltered. He said in a

perfectly ordinary voice, 'You'd better come in.'

Emma tossed her red-gold hair over one shoulder. 'I prefer to say what I have to say and then go. I have an appointment with the Kwa Zulu constabulary in Nelsburg, to report the cases of arson, harassment and malicious damage to my property for which you have recently been responsible. Before that,' she continued sweetly, 'I demand payment for all the gardening work I've already undertaken. Then I wish never to set eyes on you again!'

Jeremy went very still. 'I believe,' he said quietly, 'that we are at cross purposes. You owe me more of an explanation than that.'

'I owe you nothing,' Emma snapped. 'It's you who owes me!' She stuck out her hand. 'My payment, if you please.'

She watched a look of distaste disappear quickly behind a bland mask as Jeremy drew out his pocket book. He scribbled out a cheque and thrust it at her as though it was burning his hand . . . as it would his pocket.

Emma looked at it to verify the amount and gasped. 'But this is far, far too much!'

'Of course it isn't,' he said tightly. 'It's no less than you deserve, you abominable girl. Did you really think I would allow you to work for a pittance?'

'Yes . . . No. But you can't afford this!'

'I can afford anything I want,' he grated. 'Good day, Miss Milton.'

Emma drove into Nelsburg, deposited the money into her bank account and took herself to the Chilly Monkey for a cup of coffee. Not since her parents' death in that car accident had she felt so utterly dismal.

The Nelsburg grapevine, she reflected miserably, would have the story of their misfortunes all over the province by noon tomorrow, and Gran would be forced to endure a hundred people ringing her up to commiserate — not to mention a visit from that awful reporter at the Nelsburg Gazette.

On the other hand, if she let the matter drop they would be spared that misery. In her experience, the less one stirred matters, the sooner they died a natural death.

And Jeremy had indeed been extremely generous about payment; an admission of guilt if ever there was one. Perhaps she wouldn't go to the police after all.

Emma gulped her coffee and waited for the caffeine to kick in. Jeremy Fenner, she told herself fiercely, must be completely wiped from her mind. Even Arabella would be forbidden to speak of him again.

The Miltons would get on with their lives, rebuild their business and consign him to the compost heap, where he belonged. How arrogant could the man get? To think he imagined he could kick them off their land!

Loud voices interrupted her thoughts.

Emma peered round the potted palm next to her and gasped. Her cousin, Antonia, was yelling at someone in a most un-ladylike way.

She watched in amazement as Antonia flung down her table napkin and stood up.

'I will not be blackmailed for any more money,' she told Craig Fenner furiously. 'I don't care what you do! You can tell that stupid Emma, for all I care, you won't get another penny out of me. And you can pay for the coffee . . . ' She snatched up her handbag and flounced out.

Emma picked up her coffee mug and made her way to Craig's table. 'Tell Emma what?' she demanded.

Craig had the grace to look sheepish. 'I only wanted to wind her up. I wanted to see how far she'd go to hide her sins.'

'What sins?'

Craig sighed. 'She paid me to wreck your place and set the barn on fire. I only did it for the money, but as Jeremy said, it was a criminally stupid thing to do. I'm sorry.'

He switched on his charming smile. 'Am I forgiven? I'm leaving for Cape

Town in half-an-hour, just as soon as they've checked my tyres and such. Goodbye, Emma.'

Emma sat staring after him. It was a full ten minutes before she could rouse herself to pay for her coffee and leave.

9

Jeremy boiled himself an egg for breakfast and consumed it mechanically while his thoughts returned to the last conversation he'd had with Emma.

'Little vixen,' he muttered in between mouthfuls of toast. 'She'll find out the truth sooner or later. And when she crawls back to apologise I shall take great pleasure in sending her packing!'

He made himself a mug of coffee he didn't really want and wandered outside to see whether the goldfish had taken to their new environment in the water garden.

To his utter consternation Emma was there before him, clad as usual in one of her grubby gardening outfits.

She flung a pinch of goldfish flakes into the water. 'They seem to have settled,' she informed him in a perfectly ordinary voice, adding, 'you won't forget to feed them, will you?'

Jeremy stared back impassively. 'And good morning to you, too, Emma.'

'Oh . . . sorry. Good morning. Nice day,' she breezed.

What was wrong with the girl? Jeremy wondered. It was just as he'd first thought, she must be as crazy as a loon.

One moment she was like a demented warthog, and the next as charming as a gazelle. Here she was, airily reminding him to feed the fish just as though yesterday had never happened!

He sighed deeply. Crazy or not, he couldn't live without her. He was in for one heck of an interesting life!

Emma said suddenly, 'I've come to eat humble pie.'

'Oh?'

'Yes, and it's giving me indigestion since it's the second time.

'I know it's a lot to ask, but please accept my apology.'

Jeremy was determined to extract it

to the very last ounce. 'What for?'

'For misjudging you, yet again.'

'I am not a criminal, then? I'm not a verbal abuser of cheeky children or a greedy, unscrupulous grabber of other people's land?' he asked in mock surprise.

Emma gave a sudden grin. 'You are a very fine man, and you know it.'

'To what do I owe this sudden change of opinion?'

'I met Craig yesterday, before he left for Cape Town. He set me right. I know all about Antonia and her spiteful activities, but I can't say I understand why she did it.'

Jeremy did not enlighten her. 'And . . . ?'

Emma hesitated. 'Well, seeing as we are neighbours, I would like us to be . . . friends. If that's all right with you.'

Jeremy pretended to think. 'I don't find that satisfactory at all.'

Emma's heart sank. 'Well, I can quite see that you're angry, but it would be a pity not to preserve good neighbourly relations, as you once suggested. Besides, Arabella thinks you're the bee's knees. I've said I'm sorry and I don't know what else I can do.'

'You could marry me.'

Emma dropped the box of fish flakes. 'I beg your pardon?'

Jeremy laughed. 'I said, you could marry me, and we'll call it quits.'

Emma's mouth opened and closed again. She swallowed. 'Yes, I thought that's what you'd said.'

'I love you to distraction, Emma darling.'

'You do?' She saw the love in his eyes and all her doubts vanished.

Because she was an honest girl, she said faintly, 'I love you, too, Jeremy. But . . . well, I'll have to think about the marriage part.' How could she leave Gran to cope alone? And there was Arabella . . .

'Take all of ten minutes,' Jeremy assured her. 'I'm a patient man.'

She cast him a doubtful glance. 'Are you really very wealthy?'

His eyes gleamed with amusement. All at once he couldn't care less whether she married him for his money or not.

'Would it matter?'

'Oh, yes. I'd rather you were poor. I mean, I've never had much money and I wouldn't know what to do with it.'

'In that case, my darling, I'll give it all away.'

'Wait. There's no need to rush into things,' Emma advised prudently. 'After all, we'll need to hire a housekeeper for Gran, she couldn't manage on her own, and tennis rackets for Arabella don't come cheap.'

Jeremy's mouth twitched. 'I think I can manage.'

He had no immediate family of his own, and determined then and there to take good care of Emma's.

Her grandmother would have every comfort in her old age, and as for Arabella, she could spend weekends with them if she so wished.

Emma looked up at him and said

politely, 'Thank you for asking me. I'd like to marry you, Jeremy, and I'll try to be a good wife. You see, I fell in love with you the moment I discovered you'd shovelled all that soil from the driveway to save me the effort . . . '

She got no further, for Jeremy was pulling her into his arms and kissing her soundly. 'We'll need to hire a housekeeper for ourselves, too,' he informed her when he had breath. 'You'll be far too busy helping me landscape the camping area which I intend to build at Riverbush.'

At Emma's blank look, he explained. 'I've inherited all that grassland from my uncle. I've also been buying up as much adjacent land as I can, and plan to establish a large nature reserve where city people will be able to take a rest and enjoy the beauties of God's creation, just as we are fortunate enough to do here on a daily basis.'

She beamed. 'You've decided to take up the suggestion I made, then.'

Jeremy didn't bother to mention that

he'd been planning the enterprise for the past two years. 'Oh, definitely. I'll call it Riverbush Nature Park, and stock it with a variety of antelope and one or two other small game.' He paused. 'I thought I'd ask if Tom would be willing to help me manage the enterprise in between his farming operations.'

But Emma wasn't listening. 'We'll use indigenous plants around the hutted area,' she murmured, 'so they blend with the wildness of the surrounding veldt. We'll build a large dam and stock it with fish to attract the fish eagles, and one or two hides nearby would be nice . . . I can just see a shimmering landscape of reed-beds and water . . . oh, I have so many ideas!'

Jeremy kissed her again, a tender, lingering kiss, which set Emma's pulses racing and quite took her breath.

Love and joy welled up inside her, so much so that she could even find it within her to forgive her spiteful cousin, Antonia.

Now that she had found her own

happiness, Emma discovered that she wanted to be generous.

A small voice impinged on that happiness from the other side of the garden wall. 'He's kissing her, Peter. Do you think Jolly Jeremy is going to marry my sister?' Arabella demanded.

Jeremy lifted his head and glared at the two children observing them with great interest from the top of the anthill.

'Clear off, you kids,' he growled, 'we're having a private moment. Can't you find something else to do?'

The heads promptly disappeared.

'Come on, Peter,' Arabella was heard to suggest a moment later, 'it's getting boring around here. Let's throw some clods . . .'

THE END

We do hope that you have enjoyed reading this large print book.

Did you know that all of our titles are available for purchase?

We publish a wide range of high quality large print books including:
Romances, Mysteries, Classics
General Fiction
Non Fiction and Westerns

Special interest titles available in large print are:
The Little Oxford Dictionary
Music Book, Song Book
Hymn Book, Service Book

Also available from us courtesy of Oxford University Press:
Young Readers' Dictionary
(large print edition)
Young Readers' Thesaurus
(large print edition)

For further information or a free brochure, please contact us at:
Ulverscroft Large Print Books Ltd.,
The Green, Bradgate Road, Anstey,
Leicester, LE7 7FU, England.
Tel: (00 44) **0116 236 4325**
Fax: (00 44) **0116 234 0205**

Other titles in the
Linford Romance Library:

FUTURE PROMISE

Barbara Cowan

The huge problem of the sale of the garage, their home and livelihood, worried Morag Kinloch. Her father felt his only two options — be a taxi driver for a former apprentice or manage his estranged sister's business — demeaned him. Then the rumour about her young sister's new male lodger added to Morag's anxiety. So Gordon McEwan's reflections on their future had to wait.

RHAPSODY OF LOVE

Rachel Ford

When painter Maggie Sanderson found herself trapped in the same Caribbean hideaway as world-famous composer Steve Donellan, she was at a loss what to do. She tried to distance herself from him, but he seemed determined to make his presence felt, crashing his way around the house day and night. Was there no way she could find peace from this man, or was he going to ruin her sanity too, as he had ruined everything else?